HOW TO KILL YOUR WIFE

BY JOHN LAMB

www.jklambauthor.com

ABOUT THE BOOK

Philip Chambers is a normal man with a normal job, living a normal life in a normal house. He has a normal wife, two normal children and three normal grandchildren. His life is perfect, or so it appears.

Philip however, is not as normal as everyone thinks he is and the book title 'HOW TO KILL YOUR WIFE' says it all. Or does it?

This is a most unusual psychological thriller that will have the reader turning pages, wondering how much worse things could get and what could possibly happen next.

Copyright ©2017 John Lamb

All rights reserved. No part of this book may be reproduced, stored in a retrieval system or transmitted in any form or by any means without the prior written permission of the publishers, except by a reviewer who may quote brief passages in a review to be printed by a newspaper, magazine or journal.

NOTE FROM THE AUTHOR.

This is a complete work of fiction and all characters referred to in this book are fictitious, particularly the character of my wife and family.

Any reference or resemblance of any of the characters in this book to any family member, friend or colleague is not intentional. If anyone does take offence, well, to hell with them!

CHAPTER 1

As I stood up to address the group, the thought that crossed my mind was 'How many lies can one person tell in two minutes'.

Today I was attending one of several annual 'Personal Development Training Courses' organised by my company, which I first offered to my employees three years ago. I must confess that until this moment, I had always managed to avoid attending any of them myself, believing that these types of activities were a complete waste of time.

I had been persuaded some years ago to do something, when it was observed that there was an increasing amount of absenteeism from work. The cause of this, we were advised, was brought about by stress in the work place. So, this annual opportunity to voice feelings, frustrations and emotions had been my contribution to make 'their' lives at work more manageable. Surprisingly the results had been very positive.

It had been suggested that I ought to attend a course this year, to demonstrate that 'bonding' should involve all levels of management and employees alike. So here I am, at the beginning of the day, the 'Introductory Period' where everyone gets two minutes to introduce themselves and express what they would like to achieve from the day. I'd listened to fifteen others speak, and they had all spoken confidently and enthusiastically about who they were and their expectations, not just for the day, but for their career ambitions. I knew they were saying much of these words to ingratiate themselves in front of me, but I recognised it all for what it was.

So, it was now my turn to tell lies.

"Good morning, I'm aware you all know who I am, but for the benefit of the trainers, my name is Philip Chambers. I am passionate about the company I represent and have always sought to ensure its success, and as success only comes from those people who collectively work with me, I want to take this opportunity to thank everyone within the company for their efforts, dedication and commitment." A small round of applause followed these words with lots of nodding heads. I then continued with the personal details, which were predictably expected.

"I have been married for 27 years to my wonderful wife Jennifer, and we have two children who have always made us proud and have blessed us with three beautiful grandchildren that are a constant source of fun and pleasure.

We live in Slough, a town I find most friendly with a strong community spirit and is filled with people who are always cheerful and welcoming. Our house is a busy home, and we are lucky to have our family, and so many friends and neighbours who generously share their time and company with us.

My principal interests revolve around my family's activities, particularly those of my wife. Her devotion to the local church and many other charitable activities, allow me to involve myself in her rewarding works and I try to support her in everyway I can. Apart from her charitable activities, Jennifer is a wonderful cook and one of my daily pleasures is returning home in the evening to be treated to one of her culinary delights. I think you can see the result of her skills," I patted my slightly corpulent belly to demonstrate the effects of being married to a wife who was skilled in the kitchen, which made my audience laugh.

"Apart from my involvement with my wonderful family, I enjoy a little DIY around the house and tending the plants in the garden. My other interest, and my true passion, is rugby. Having played it as a boy I cannot resist going to watch matches, particularly the Internationals, so if any of you wish at anytime to endear yourself and progress your careers, tickets for Twickenham to watch England would certainly help." That caused more laughter.

"I think my two minutes is almost up, so I would like to conclude by expressing my enthusiasm for what we are going to experience and learn today. I believe, and hope that we will all leave with new attitudes and skills that will be the start of many enlightening, life changing thoughts and attitudes, allowing both our professional and personal lives to be fulfilled. Thank you." There was some more applause as I sat down.

We then had coffee and biscuits before a day of very odd exercises, in cringingly awkward situations followed.

Diary Note – Monday morning. On the train. Feeling quite 'Empowered' following Friday's Personal Development

Course. I also feel surprisingly enthusiastic with my 'Life Changing' decisions this session has helped me 'manifest'. Their training booklet 'THE MECHANICS OF LIFE', is an inspiration and I have adopted it as my bible. "Small steps well planned." So, thanks to the trainers for a truly enlightening day. I'm not very sure about the need to keep a diary note to record thoughts, feelings and emotions for the next month, but if that's what it takes, who am I to argue.

I didn't think I'd feel so positive this morning after the gruelling weekend I've just endured. And that it is Monday. I particularly dislike Mondays, not because everybody seems especially miserable on a Monday, I quite like that, no, it's that moment when I get home after work and smell the Shepherd's Pie that Jennifer presents every Monday night for dinner. How is it that a woman can search the shops for the finest, freshest and most expensive organic ingredients and create a masterpiece of greyish brown, watery, tasteless shit, covered with a slimy, glutinous topping of inedible potatoes, is beyond me. If it happened once, you could have a bit of a laugh about it and order a takeaway, but to offer this up every Monday night for 27 years is just inexcusable. I think the fucking bitch does it on purpose.

Oh, the trains arrived.

As I step off the train into the fresh air, my thoughts reflect on the journey; the overheated air of the carriage, the smell of anxiety, stress and sweat always turns my stomach and makes me wonder why I bother travelling First Class. I don't think these bastards even bother washing themselves in the morning, just some underarm deodorant and a quick spray of 'Febreze' on Friday's clothes seem to be the order of the day. Myself, I always take great care, showering, shaving, making sure the toilet seat is put down and brushing my teeth. One thing I am most particular about, is laying out my clothes the evening before in readiness for a punctual start to my routine of the morning. I started this evening preparation when I discovered one morning, to my horror, that Jennifer was only ironing the front of my shirts. When I asked her about this, she simply explained that since I never took my jacket off, even during the summer, it was a waste of time. Hardly the point, she knows I like everything to be just right, now I must iron the rest of the shirt myself every night before going to bed. Bloody woman, Christ only knows what she does all day, 27 years we've been married, and it's gone downhill since the passions of the first few years disappeared with the arrival of our two children. What a collection of selfish, thoughtless fucking brats they turned out to be. I always wanted to give them a smack when they were at the peak of their grizzling, but Jennifer didn't believe in smacking and chose to use bribery as a means of control. Myself, I was always given a 'good hiding' when I misbehaved, and it hasn't done me any harm.

Anyway, the little darlings are in their 20's now, but has the whining and demanding stopped? No, and we only see them when they want something, like last weekend. Susanne, our eldest daughter, who has blessed us with two evil, rude little turds we fondly call grandchildren, had suggested they come over for "a nice family day" on Sunday. "That would be fantastic," Jennifer had replied. I just thought, "How much does she want this time?"

Sunday, 10 o'clock they all duly arrived, the two brats, my fat arsed daughter and the star of the show, Mr Right himself, our son in law, who knows everything and does nothing, a proper righteous wanker. And who was right? Well me, of course. They hadn't been there 20 minutes and, bless the grandbrats, it was just sufficient enough time to break a vase, a glass and trample the flowerbed to oblivion, before the tears appeared in Susanne's eyes. She explained how much she hated to ask, but their car had failed its MOT and they needed to borrow some money to buy a new one. I love this word 'borrow', why doesn't she just say, "Give us some money", borrowing implies that we would be repaid, which has never happened in the many previous occasions. Before I get a chance to tell her that she's got no chance, Jennifer's already got our chequebook out and is doling out the money.

Diary note – Arrived at work, still feeling inspired. Usual stuff. Secretary Valerie looks good, nice legs, pity she has to open her mouth and speak though.

Lunchtime – My thoughts are really beginning to crystallise. There has been a lot of discussion around the office about the Personal Development Training Course. Everyone who went believes it has changed their thinking; it had been a benefit to them in how they dealt with people, particularly their work colleagues and how they manage the pressures of work. I agreed with them, I likewise have realised that things need to change and what I must do to make these changes happen.

So, I have decided to kill Jennifer. If I'm rid of her, I can be rid of the rest of the family as well; the grand-brats, my two money grabbing children and my self-opinionated bag of a mother in law, Edith; she's either going straight into a home or I might kill her as well. But I intend to follow the training booklet and make these changes through the "Small steps, well planned," advice.

The problem with this killing business is that it needs to be well thought through and executed so I can appear completely innocent and act out the distraught husband role. I shouldn't probably be writing this in a diary, but I do need to make notes somewhere to help develop these plans and consider the consequences.

Packed up and left the office to catch the train home. Uneventful day, no unusual emotional or stressful issues to record.

I'm sure I can smell the dreaded Shepherd's Pie as soon as I got off the train at the station in Slough. Why did we ever come to live in the dump that is Slough? Well, when I say we, I mean Jennifer. She decided we ought to live close to her mother, "To keep an eye on her" after the old bitch had driven her husband to an early grave. They say he died of a heart attack, personally I think he just lost the will to live after being served Shepherd's Pie every Monday night for more than 40 years. This incredible recipe is one I believe, that's been lovingly passed down through generations to Jennifer.

Slough was not my first choice of town to live in, neither was the choice of our house, which now looms in front of me as I approach. A four bedroomed, post war, detached shithole, in a drab street with annoying neighbours, all pleasantly situated in Slough. Could things be worse? I'm sure an Estate Agent could talk it up and make it sound better, but this is home for me.

"Hi darling, I'm home", I announce as I enter the hallway. White ceiling, magnolia walls and a deep blue plush carpet that still holds its pile and colour, apart from the track from the front door to the kitchen where many little angelic feet have trod in their eagerness to snatch and break something without first wiping their feet.

"Something smells nice". I know, I'm being 'two faced', but hey, I'm going to kill the woman, I don't want to add discourtesy to my crime; that would be rude. My mother taught me always to be polite and courteous, she was a formidable woman. If I'd had a sister who had asked my mother for some money, she would have had something considerably more substantial in her hand than a chequebook. My mother was a large woman from the Scottish Highlands, brought up on a diet of porridge and frugal Presbyterianism. Generosity and kindness were not words that appeared in any of the dictionaries she was familiar with, and certainly could not be used to describe her personality. I don't think she even knew what a chequebook was, she just had her purse that was used so often the hinges had rusted. She was a great cook and specialised in thin, watery soups with plenty of that pearl barley children love so much.

"It's your favourite, Shepherd's Pie" announces Jennifer.

I fucking hate Mondays.

CHAPTER 2

Diary Note: - Feel a little queasy this morning, I didn't sleep well, my mind was too active. Went through a few different ideas to achieve my objective and, as is usual with night-time thoughts, they're not very practical or achievable in the morning light of day. The concept of one that I do recall, was quite good in that I 'killed two birds with one stone'; the two 'birds' being Jennifer and her mother. Further positive thought needs to be given. Just arrived at work, feel a little tense.

I reflect over the rather ridiculous, but most enjoyable dream like action from the night before, it's always incredible, you have unending skills in these semi wakeful moments. This plan, and others that had originated in my mind, a mind that has no practical knowledge at all, I don't think I even have a screwdriver in the house, I certainly cannot recall ever using one. But in my dream, I have carefully altered the gas pipe in my Mother in law, Edith's house, and have rigged up an ignition system to cause an explosion when the front door of the house is opened. It's wonderful how so little goes wrong in an imaginary world. Jennifer duly arrives, opens the door and BOOM, the whole house explodes.

What a vision, I see the wicked witch herself in flames, flailing about in her armchair, eyes wide open, her hair completely scorched off, but her mouth still screeching with obscenities as to my parents' marital status. Jennifer just quietly blazes away in the porch, unable to compete with her mother's diatribe.

While all this is going on, I'm sitting in my office; calm, smartly dressed, diligently working to support an ever demanding and needy family, when Valerie enters my office. Valerie has always had a body that was worth more than a glance, but in my dream her attributes were considerably enlarged and only delicately covered by gossamer like clothing. I could see she was enjoying the sensation as my eyes touched her sensuous curves and her normally well concealed erogenous zones. With a very inviting and flirtatious voice, she tells me that there are some policemen asking to see me.

Detective Inspector Tracey and Detective Sergeant Catchem, a formidable police duo, enter my office.

"Sir, I am afraid I have some rather bad news, there has been an accident at number 2, Coven Street, Slough. I am sorry, but we believe that both your wife and her mother have been killed in the accident."

I fall back into my seat, the expression on my face is a mask of shock, and with acting skills that belonged on a Shakespearian stage, I allowed tears to flow down my face as I wail. "Not Jennifer, not my Jennifer, it can't be true".

The DI continued, "I know this is very distressing for you sir, but I must ask you to accompany us to the mortuary to identify the bodies."

My imagined trip to the morgue was unbelievable; my acting skills deserved at least a BAFTA, pretending to stumble as we enter and being supported by the delightful DS Catchem - I even managed a 'careless hand' movement across her breast! The smell of burnt flesh, scorched hair and clothes, tantalise my nostrils and as the sheets are removed, a joyous vision is revealed as the blackened, hairless forms of Jennifer and Edith are there for me to behold.

Aren't dreams wonderful!!

CHAPTER 3

Diary note: - Tuesday – No emotional issues to report. Returned home from the office and was greeted by Jennifer and the robust smell of braised liver and onions. Jennifer always cooks liver and onions with gravy on a Tuesday night. In the early days of our marriage, Tuesday night started out as her 'surprise night' and I remember well the first time she cooked liver and onions, 27 years ago, on a Tuesday night, and it was a surprise, a fucking awful surprise, but a surprise nevertheless. I blame myself for not saying something sooner, but I always hoped that she would get sick of it herself and cook something different. I never really wanted to risk asking Jennifer to change this dish from her culinary routine; the liver and onions with 'surprise' gravy wasn't good, but she was capable of cooking far worse.

I was surprised to see my son, David sitting morosely at the kitchen table, his mother making comforting sounds whilst stroking his hand. I put on my 'don't worry, we're here for you,' sincere face, and joined them at the table, waiting to hear how much this current cause for concern was going to cost. "David's lost his job" was all the information I was given by Jennifer.

When people use expressions like "I've lost my job" one part of you thinks, 'What do you mean you've lost your job, how do you lose something like that, have you searched for it? Where was the last place you saw it, you careless arsehole? Do you really mean that you've been sacked because you're a lazy waste of space?'

Another part of you thinks 'That's not fair, he's really very upset and has come to you and his family for love and comfort during a difficult time.'

'What a load of rubbish' that first inner voice challenges, 'his understanding of the phrase 'love and comfort' has the same meaning as ' financial support'

'Stop'. This is another voice that exists, the voice of moderation, the voice of reason, the voice I believe to be the 'real me', Philip Chambers, that mediates between the other two extreme voices. I used to be a little concerned that maybe I had some psychological problem, hearing these voices in my head, but now I'm sure everyone has conversations with themselves. However, it is difficult to be certain, you cannot really ask a friend, "So how many voices do you hear in your head?" this would certainly reserve you a place on the bus to the funny farm.

David losing his job is not a new or unusual phenomenon, but we always have to suffer the melodramatics. For all he got an opportunity to grumble at length to us over the injustice of his situation, I do think he regretted taking this opportunity as Jennifer began sharing our supper with him and he remembered it was Tuesday night. I cannot begin to describe my pleasure, firstly by the fact that my portion of this delightful dish was very much reduced, but secondly, the sight of my son's face as Jennifer carefully placed two large slices of this robust organ on his plate with her special 'surprise' sauce, which tonight was proudly introduced as a 'carrot, honey and garlic jus'. I was surprised initially, and my mind was intrigued with this rather interesting sounding gravy, however, I was reassured, when it was applied to the liver, that it was the usual watery grey dressing that I was accustomed to but with some very small flecks of orange in it. Happiness came in abundance watching David enjoy his meal.

Jennifer suggested that David and his family move in with us until he found another job. I surprised both of them by offering to help with his house rent instead. My God! the choice of having David, the tart-in-law and their screaming hell-child living with us, or simply pay over some money, wasn't a difficult decision, plus their presence would completely ruin some of the 'life changing' plans I'm working on.

CHAPTER 4

Diary note: Wednesday - Good day at the office, the team performed with their usual efficiency. No dramas, no emotional stress, good camaraderie. Valerie was wearing black today, not sure why I noticed this.

It's funny how the smallest of things often bring memories flooding back. As I exited Slough Station on this Wednesday evening, my eyes were caught by the sight of an elderly, and rather portly woman kneeling on her porch step doing something mundane, but the sight of her brown shoes and the large roundness of her buttocks draped in a heavy skirt, brought back an image from my childhood and made my face grimace.

My mother was a staunch Presbyterian and part of her churchly duties was to clean the presbytery, the minister's residence, on a

Monday, Wednesday and Friday afternoon. As part of my duties, I was expected to go to the presbytery after school on these days to carry out several menial tasks, 'In the service of God', by helping to carry home the many pieces of cleaning equipment my mother had required for her duties. It always seemed to be raining on Mondays, Wednesdays and Fridays.

The presbytery was not a place anybody visited out of choice, only ever in the dutiful service of God and his representative on earth, the minister. It was a large, austere, grey building, always dark and grim; on the few sunny days that I do remember, the curtains and shutters were immediately closed to prevent the evil light from entering and bleaching any part of the drab, grey interior. There was an almost liquid feel to the atmosphere within the house, the coldness, the dampness and the staleness of the air seemed to hold you with arms of oppression and fear. It had a smell that was impossible to clearly define, there was a hint of beeswax, a hint of mildew and then this other unidentifiable, overwhelming smell that as a child I thought smelled of death and decay.

The presbytery terrified me; it was always so quiet, any sounds that were made or permeated from the outside, were quickly devoured by this formidable structure. The only sound that could be heard on the days I went, emanated from the minister's office. The door was always closed, and the sounds were of muffled voices speaking in deep, reverent tones. On a Monday afternoon, the minister met with the elders of the church to pray and give thanks for the offerings that had been collected from the congregation at the Sunday services. These offerings had been carefully counted and recorded before being deposited at the bank by Mr Luke, the churchwarden. Only the minister and the church elders knew how much had been collected, only they knew what purpose these monies would be used for, only they knew anything, and nobody would ever dare raise a question for fear of immortal damnation. They knew their place and their duties, and they knew the duties of the parishioners. The parishioners knew their duties, which were twofold. Firstly, they had to go to church at least once on a Sunday, so they could be lambasted with threats of hell and damnation. Secondly, fill the collection plates with money before they left.

I was terrified of the minister, the elders and the church, I constantly worried about going to hell for some minor offence that was beyond my control.

On Sunday, the children were only subjected to first hour of the full two-hour service that the adults had to endure. Children were granted this release, so they may attend Sunday school. We learnt so much there about Christians, Good Samaritans, feeding the 5000, but most of all about Baby Jesus and his Virgin Mother. We didn't know what a Virgin Mother was and if anyone made the mistake of asking difficult questions like "What's a Virgin Mother?" they were made to stand in the corner with their hands on their head. Even at this young age, the 'evil' voice in my head would demand answers to questions like these and I often vocalised them before I could stop myself. I usually had plenty of time to study the peeling lincrusta wallpaper that revealed the mould on the damp plaster below, in the dark corner.

I was twelve before I discovered what a Virgin Mother was, 400 hours of attending Sunday school and yet it only took Peter Stiles, a new school friend, five minutes to explain the natural relationships between a man and woman. I felt very distressed with this explanation and was almost sick as I walked home, I couldn't get the image of my mother and father fornicating in the graphic way that Peter had described. I was convinced that I would certainly be going to hell now.

This information and many other important life changing snippets of knowledge, were passed on to me at this age. Starting 'Big School' exposed you to a great variety of children from different backgrounds. My 'education' at the hands of the Church of England and Catholic children was dramatic. My perpetual fear of going to hell didn't seem to exist within these two groups. The Church of England children didn't seem to believe or care about anything religious and only became interested in Baby Jesus at Christmas time, when they would go overboard re-enacting all the events surrounding his birth, particularly the bit where he received gifts. Obviously as gold, frankincense and myrrh were in short supply, bicycles and toys of every shape and size had become the representations of these royal gifts.

The Catholics on the other hand, did seem to take their religion much more seriously, but were relaxed in the knowledge that they could almost do anything they liked, or commit any offence without fear of going to hell. They seemed to believe that God was very forgiving and as long as they confessed their sins every week to the priest and did their penance, the slate was 'wiped clean' and could commence another week of sinning.

And so, at the age of twelve on a Monday afternoon, I entered the presbytery after school to do my usual duties. The hallway held the same oppressive atmosphere and the silence was only broken by the deep vocal murmurs vibrating through the heavy door of the presbytery office. Pausing with indecision, one voice urging me to listen at the door, another pleading for me to commence my humble chores, I finally took two tiptoed paces forward, before my eyes were suddenly distracted by a movement on the stairs. Turning, I saw a vision that has stayed with me my whole life, a vision so dreadful that I was unable to move or drag my eyes from the sight.

There on the stairs, not ten feet away, kneeling and quietly washing the staircase was my mother, but an image of her in a position and state of dress that I was not familiar with. My mother was always a very large woman, not in height but in every other dimension, I had always been aware of her bulk as she regularly used her size as a formidable tool when handing out her punishments, as she regularly did, even sometimes for the most trivial of mistakes or accidents. She did not believe her actions were 'punishments', but more a compassionate guidance to help with my education of how to behave in society. I learnt to appreciate these acts of selfless love, as she delivered her words of wisdom between the strokes of the ruler across my hands or her belt across my buttocks. Advice such as "This hurts me more than it hurts you" or "This is for your own good" or "God punishes sinners and my hand is guided by him".

But today, on this Monday afternoon, I really appreciated the enormity of this woman. My eyes were fixed. Her arse was enormous and was completely exposed as her skirt had been caught in the heavy elastic waistband of her pants, her only shred of decency. I couldn't use the word panties or knickers to describe her undergarment as both words evoke images of scantiness or frivolity; even the word pants sound too evocative. Her arse, adorned in this very tired, over washed pale cream garment, was a horrendous sight in itself, but then there were the detailed images that no 12-year-old boy should ever be exposed to. The pants were split for a length of about 6 inches, exposing her arsehole. This arsehole was not as I had imagined an arsehole would look like, it was hairy for a start, and had some protruding pink fleshy bits as decorations.

The horror did not end there, exiting this somewhat flawed undergarment, were her legs, huge chunks of pale white wobbling flesh, mottled and streaked with large, greeny/blue veins. The vision concluded with the sight of her stockings, which appeared only to start at her knees and down, finally to her stout brown shoes.

My paralysis disappeared as this monolithic hulk moved suddenly down one step to aid the cleaning process, my eyes went to the floor as my feet silently returned me to the relative safety of the entrance porch. I stood there, staring at the floor, in a state of shock, until I was suddenly brought back to full awareness as my mother slapped me across the side of my head, leaving one of my ears painfully ringing. As my senses returned I was relieved to observe that her wardrobe malfunction had been corrected.

In my prayers I forgave her but try as I might I could not erase the images from my mind, and today, standing on the concourse of Slough station, seeing this lady kneeling on her steps with her stout brown shoes, brought back the childhood memory of that brief moment at the bottom of the stairs, on that Monday afternoon in the presbytery.

CHAPTER 5

Diary note:

Arrived home to be greeted with several different images and aromas. The most pungent was of course our usual Wednesday night dinner of 'macaroni and cheese bake'. The smell of burnt cheese merged with the smell of cardboard boxes and unwashed, second-hand, mildewed clothes, which all combined to create a perfume that was not particularly welcoming, and I wished I'd gone for a drink with my colleagues after work; I would then have missed the lady on the steps at the station and avoided those disturbing memories, memories that continued with my homecoming. Feel annoyed and upset.

Jennifer had obviously been busy for most of the day. For weeks now, the house had progressively filled with empty cardboard boxes and black bin bags filled with other people's junk. The boxes and the junk were now well on their way to being combined, ready for delivery to the church hall for Saturdays jumble sale. I gave a mumbled greeting to demonstrate my irritation at this unwelcome, but unfortunately, not unusual intrusion to our domestic arrangements, and went through to the kitchen to prepare some drinks. Whilst pouring two glasses of wine, my mind drifted to the memory of why I have this phobia about the smell of cardboard boxes and second-hand clothes. It is partly to do with that 'Monday afternoon vision on the stairs' and partly to do with a more dramatic event that happened some three months later. Like today, it was a Wednesday afternoon and, as I entered the Presbytery to start my routine chores, I could sense a lighter, less forbidding atmosphere than normal.

Wednesday afternoon was usually the time the minister met with the elders to discuss, with much passion, care and love, the activities in Parish and the continuing well-being of the parishioners. But today the minister's office door was ajar, and the house was silent, except for a very strange, muffled, whimpering sound whose source was difficult to place, it was certainly distant and initially I believed it was coming from the office. Gingerly, and thinking there was perhaps an animal trapped, I crept across the hallway, my senses sharp and focused with nervousness, I had never entered the sanctity of the minister's office but had always been desperately curious and had imagined the room holding all sorts of instruments of torture, whips and canes to help instruct the practitioners in the ways of God.

The door was open sufficient for a boy to put his head in, and while contemplating this daring action, I looked through the narrow space into the office and observed the dark wooden floor, dark wooden wall panelling, ending at a height of some three feet above the floor before the cream painted plastered walls continued to the high, cream painted plastered ceiling. My head entered the opening and my nose was assaulted by that indescribable smell, which now seemed to take on a much more pungent strength. The key musty notes that permeated the house were now strongly reinforced with that other smell, a cold, lonely, forbidding odour that almost made me turn and run. My determination to satisfy my curiosity however, overcame my fear and my body followed my head to enter the doorway. My eyes scanned the room with anticipation, excitement and curiosity, but all my imaginings were immediately crushed by a bland vision of plainness.

The dark wooden floor, the dark wooden wall panelling, the cream walls and the cream ceiling were in fact the only decorative features of the room, which was illuminated by a slit of daylight entering through a partially shuttered window, sufficient for me to admire the basic furniture; a collection of ancient and well used hard wooden chairs surrounding a large wooden, highly polished table, which was unmistakably the source of the beeswax odour. The only other article of furniture in the room was the ministers desk, another large plain piece of brown furniture that supported a block of white paper and a pen, nothing else, no thumbscrews, no sharp instruments, no canes, no rulers, nothing!

The only other adornments in the room were mounted on the walls. The first was a large wooden cross, again in dark wood, which supported a magnificent carving of Jesus. His head tilted towards heaven, his blue eyes searching for understanding, the crown of brutal thorns had punctured his milk white skin to allow his scarlet blood to run. His pale, emaciated body hung from outstretched arms and crossed feet that had been cruelly nailed to prevent his escape but allowed the introduction of more crimson decorative colour to this enlightening and uplifting image for all Christians to behold and worship.

To the left of Jesus and immediately central to the desk were the other two decorative items, both embroidered panels in colours that complimented these drab surroundings. It was the words that brought the panels to life. These were the 'mantras' for every Presbyterian minister to begin his Sunday sermon with, embroidered in an ancient and decorative script. On the first was: -

"For the wrath of God is revealed from heaven against all the unholiness and unrighteousness of man"

- Romans 1:18

And on the second: -

"I will execute great vengeance on them with wrathful rebukes, then they will know that I am the Lord"
- EZEKIEL 25:17

Before my thoughts could dwell further on these parables of virtue, a groaning from somewhere behind and above distracted me. The sound was certainly not from the minister's office, which had now lost all interest to me. I retraced my steps into the hallway and as I approached the bottom of the staircase, I spotted one of my mother's brown shoes carelessly resting on its side on one of the steps, halfway up the stairs. The shoe and the surrounding steps were covered in dusty debris and for a moment I wondered if God had executed his great vengeance on her and the shoe and this dust was all that remained of her.

The muffled whimpering from above commenced once more, now much louder and closer and with a growing anxiousness, I quietly climbed the stairs to the half landing. From this vantage point I could see and smell, piles of cardboard boxes, old clothes, books and small ornaments, neatly stacked in piles on the large landing floor. I could also see a wooden ladder reaching up to an opening in the ceiling to access the attic, then, as my focus was directed to the ceiling, a slight movement in the corner of my eye made me look almost immediately above to finally discover the source of the muffled sounds.

Several emotions flooded through me as I stared upwards. Shock, embarrassment and anger being the principal ones as I observed the lower torso and legs of my mother protruding from the ceiling above. I knew it was my mother as I recognised the one remaining stout brown shoe still attached to her left foot, I recognised the wrinkled stockings that ended at her knees, I recognised the pale, flabby white legs with their blue/green decorative lines that appeared like strange tattoos, I recognised the pale cream undergarment, taking some solace as I observed that the split that had exposed sights and caused me so much distress the first time, had been repaired with course stitches made with a heavy brown thread. I recognised her brown skirt that was rucked up and tangled amongst the broken wooden ceiling laths, these same laths and nails that now supported and trapped her in their embrace.

My shock and embarrassment were now entirely replaced with anger and indignation. How dare she expose herself in this way? It had taken me some time to forgive, and I had genuinely forgiven her for the incident some months earlier, however, to discover this image for a second time, again in the presbytery, the earthly representative of God's home, was unforgivable and I believed my anger was a signal that it was I who must deliver a "Wrathful rebuke".

Climbing the rest of the stairs, negotiating my way through the cardboard boxes and the musty smelling detritus awaiting packaging, I clambered up the wooden ladders and entered the dimly lit attic space. A single light bulb cast shadows across more piles of books, boxes and trunks that awaited my mother's attention, and there she was, or rather, there was the top half of her. Her eyes turned in my direction and a warm, loving smile appeared on her face. I had never seen this look on her face before and I had difficulty in interpreting its meaning, deciding finally that it was too sinister and unnatural to belong on my mother's face. Her lips moved, and she whispered,

"Philip, thank the lord you are here, please go and get help, quickly".

I knew then for certain that my mother had been possessed, very few of the words she used were familiar to me. Her expression that she was thankful to see me and her direct use of the word "please", had never ever been used in my presence. The thought of seeking help and allowing others to see my mother in this dire state of undress, would not be something she would wish, so with a firm resolve and a strong belief I approached her and explained.

"No mother, you need to do as I say."

Her eyes locked on mine and we exchanged unblinking stares. I placed my hands on her shoulders and began to push downwards whilst I continued to explain, in a comforting way, that,

"This is going to hurt me more than it hurts you" and "I'm only doing this for your own good". Our eyes never parted as her decent began into the stairwell void below. It began slowly at first, with the sounds of snapping and cracking as the brittle ceiling laths relinquished their hold, dust rose up to form motes in the feeble light. Our eyes remained locked as her downward movement turned into free flight, she became like a floating angel drifting weightless in the air, slowly and remorselessly downwards, our eyes exchanging understanding in this brief and memorable moment of pure silence.

I have often reflected on this 'brief moment', what was she thinking? As she first began her decent I'm sure her mind was clouded with fury. I could read from her eyes that her thoughts, had they been vocalised, would have said.

"You're going to be eating pearl barley soup for the rest of your life you little bastard".

However, towards the final part of her decent, I could see that her thoughts changed more towards the spiritual, her face and eyes revealed the words, "Fucking Hell" that gave a clear indication of her belief to her next destination.

Like all memorable moments, they often end abruptly, and this ending was certainly abrupt. With a huge sound that combined a great 'Whooosh' of air with a hefty 'thrump' and a loud 'crack', my mother landed on the ornately decorated, but well-polished, balustrade rail with the middle of her back. Despite this, her eyes never left mine and she continued to stare, albeit now with a blankness, as she emulated a gymnast with twitching feet and hands performing 'the crab' position.

I descended the attic stairs, dusting myself down, straightening my school tie and checking that the rest of my school uniform was clean, before walking down the stairs to where my mother now rested. I was impatient to ensure that she was properly dressed, and her modesty was in no way compromised by her current position, I replaced her shoes and pulled her skirt down to below her knees before I finally decided to summon help.

"Emergency, which service do you require?" The operator demanded after I had dialled 999. I nearly replied that I had been thinking of changing to either a Church of England or a Catholic service, but I focused my attention and replied that I wasn't sure, but I definitely did not require a fire engine. The operator patiently asked me to explain what had happened and so I described how I had arrived at the presbytery to help my mother, as I always did on a Monday, Wednesday and Friday afternoon, and as it was Wednesday today, I was obviously at the presbytery. I believed my mother had been emptying the attic of stuff ready to be sent to those who had greater need of it, possibly poor black people in Africa, but couldn't be exactly sure. The operator, who had been silent up to this point, suddenly, and rudely I thought, interrupted by firmly demanding why I was calling the emergency services. I told her I was trying my best to explain the situation to her, but I was feeling rather anxious and afraid. The operator apologised and more patiently asked me to tell her what had happened, so I continued and told her how my mother had been looking forward to doing this particular job as she loved helping the minister and the church in its efforts to bring comfort to those who are poor and in need. Finally, I concluded my detailed explanation of how I had arrived at the presbytery to discover my mother lying over the banisters and that, although I hadn't checked thoroughly, I was convinced she was dead.

There was then quite a long silent pause across the phone line, I think the operator had lapsed into silent disinterest, but as my diatribe concluded and my words sunk into the operators understanding, her enthusiasm for her job quickly returned as she realised the severity of the situation.

"Oh! You'll need the police and ambulance, don't you worry dearie, they're on their way, stay on the phone and we can continue to talk while we wait for them to arrive."

"Thank you", I replied "but I think we'll need the services of an emergency builder as well because the ceiling has really been damaged and it won't be long before the minister returns and he's not going to be pleased if he comes home to find that my mother has damaged his house."

What a kind and sympathetic woman the operator was, she tried to hold my attention by telling me that she had gone to the seaside at Dunbar for her summer holidays and asked me to tell her where I had gone for my holidays. I thought about this for some moments and was about to explain that I had never had a summer holiday away from home because there were always chores to do but was interrupted by the arrival of the police who took the phone off me. They were also very kind and supportive. It was however, the arrival home of the minister that was the greatest surprise to me, he never mentioned the damage and mess, instead, and with a very 'holy' expression and a patronising manner, he made everyone stand still, with their heads bowed, while he said a prayer expressing the mysterious ways of the Lord and only he, in his infinite wisdom, knew the reason for the departure of this wonderful and saintly woman.

It was at this moment I felt much closer to God as I realised that it was only Him and me who knew the truth! Quite a memorable day.

CHAPTER 6

Diary note:

The macaroni and cheese was dreadful. Sitting in the kitchen drinking wine. Jennifer's still packing boxes, so I cannot even sit and watch the television. I have been giving a great deal of thought to my 'project' and need to record the objectives and issues surrounding the potential pitfalls for future consideration and review.

Objectives: -

1). To kill Jennifer

2). Not to be held accountable for her death.

Together the combination of these two objectives are considerably more difficult to achieve than I first imagined. I have discovered, by reading different sites on the Internet, much of the information that I need to be mindful of. A key discovery is that the primary suspect in any wife killing is always the husband, and their suspicions are usually correct. The police consider three key points in establishing guilt: -

a) MOTIVE: - Jennifer has a large life insurance policy. For all the world, Jennifer and I have a 'perfect', happy and stable relationship, so I'm certain an investigation wouldn't consider the fact that she can't cook and is the most boring women on the planet as a motive for murder. Nevertheless, the insurance money would be considered a great motivator and would give them a reason to look closely.

b) OPPORTUNITY: - There are two options to consider: -

- *I am in the vicinity of her death and therefore the evidence would have to point towards either an accident or the action of someone else, or*

- *I can demonstrate that I am elsewhere when she is killed.*

c) PHYSICAL EVIDENCE: - This is a problem. I have watched many of the forensic evidence programmes on the TV, Jennifer loves them, and between CCTV cameras recording everyone's movements, their location through their mobile phone and working with minute traces of DNA and statements from eye witnesses, the list goes on and makes it very difficult for an amateur like myself to fulfil the simple objective of killing your wife and getting away with it.

I'm going to bed, I need to give this a lot more thought.

Sleep escapes me. I can hear Jennifer still moving about, shifting boxes and talking to herself about which stall should have which box; who gives a fuck, as I wrestle beneath the sheets to find the perfect position that will induce slumber. Lying on my back, my arms by my side, I ask myself for the 100th time, why I want things to change. Jennifer and I have never been 'passionately' in love, more of a passionate fondness that developed into a convenient, comfortable, easy routine.

Unfortunately, as with most marriages, the passion quite quickly disappeared. This disappearance occurred with the changes that naturally take place, or so I understand, with the arrival of children. Any love that you may have had, any attention you may have lavished upon each other and time you spent together as lovers, becomes diluted or even washed into oblivion with the arrival of children. I can understand why some couples remain childless, they have obviously experienced having children in 'another lifetime' and have an instinct to avoid making the same mistake a second time. This, I think must be Jennifer and I's 'first lifetime' experience as I'm certain we wouldn't have repeated the experience again.

Our early life together was perfect bliss and harmony. We had met on Brighton Pier when Jennifer literally fell into my arms. I was having a week's holiday, basically doing nothing. As I was walking onto the pier, I couldn't help noticing a couple having a heated argument, they stood almost nose-to-nose, with much finger pointing and waving. My curiosity encouraged me to slow my pace and alter my direction, so I could pass close by them to hear better the exchange. As I got close, Jennifer exclaimed,

"You are such a fucking arsehole" and spun on her heals to illustrate that this was to be the final word on the matter. Unfortunately, one of her 'spinning heals' didn't, and with an undignified yelp of pain she lost her balance and fell into my arms. It was love at first grope for me. I had always been attracted to plump women with large breasts and within a fraction of a second of our first meeting I had established that Jennifer fitted both criteria.

I helped her to a bench seat and recovered her shoe, the "fucking arsehole" having left in an unsympathetic tantrum. She had hurt her ankle, which quickly became very swollen and prevented her being able to replace the shoe or putting any weight on it. My mind quickly analysed; I could either go in search of the missing boyfriend and leave him to sort everything out, or I could tell her I was going to get some help from the First Aider, then just go home and not get involved, or I could be gentile, kind and chivalrous and help her in the hope that I might get a shag later for my efforts. Well, and only I know this, I actually chose the First Aider/going home never to return option.

Home was a small bedsit only a 10-minute walk away from the pier, more than enough time for an argument to break out in my mind, one thought supporting the chivalrous concept and the other supporting the belief that a shag would result, both arguing against my sensible self's decision not to return at all. So, after a few minutes of sitting thinking, I put my half drank bottle of beer back in the fridge and left the flat, retracing my steps to find that Jennifer was still waiting patiently, trustingly and helplessly on the bench.

"No luck with the First Aiders I'm afraid, so my only suggestion is that I help you to get home, where do you live?" I asked.

"Slough" she replied with a grateful look on her face.

"Slough?" I questioned, just to be certain.

"Yes, Slough" she confirmed without any hint of an apology.

I mentally rebuked both my alter egos for their stupidity; I should always trust my own first instinct.

I helped Jennifer off the pier and onto the promenade where I sat her on a seat close to the road edge and returned to the bedsit, finished my beer, still rebuking myself for allowing my better judgement to be compromised in this way, collected my car and went to pick up the invalid.

My car, a pale blue, four-year-old Ford Cortina, belonged to my employer, Elliot and Baker, a local insurance agency that specialised in house, contents and car insurance. My working life there was pretty mundane, perpetually filling in forms and trying to persuade customers of the need to take out insurance, from which I eked out a living on commission. The car was one of the principal reasons for me taking the job, not that I had many choices as jobs were still hard to come by.

Helping Jennifer into the front seat we set off on our journey to Slough. Our conversation was fun, I enjoyed her company and the drive passed quite quickly. She told me that she had just finished her diploma in office studies and was enjoying a few weeks holiday before starting work as an 'Office Assistant', a job which I thought sounded very much like that of a secretary, but I said nothing as she seemed to think it was a senior position. Her boyfriend had suggested they have a day in Brighton, avoiding the weekend crowds by coming on a Monday.

"What were you arguing about?" I asked following the logic of our conversation.

"He wanted us to book into a hotel and stay overnight, I reminded him that we'd promised my Mother that we'd be back in time for dinner and he just got so rude and angry. He and my Mother don't like each other, she's not too easy to get along with, but she is my Mother and he had no right to call her names", she stopped and when I glanced over I could see that she was upset, and tears were forming in her eyes. Despite this I had to ask.

"What names?"

She stayed silent for some time and I was unsure if she was just going to ignore my question, when she suddenly blurted out with a sob.

"He said that she was a fucking rude, evil bitch and if he ever had to eat from her cauldron again it would still be too soon." I found it very difficult not to laugh, but I should have heeded this early warning notice, the ex-boyfriend's description turned out to be a great understatement.

Jennifer was obviously very upset, so I gently changed the subject and our conversation moved onto more routine topics, schooldays, holidays we'd had in the past, favourite places. I discovered that Jennifer had spent most of her childhood holidays in Devon in a caravan her parents had owned, she told of these memories, how she'd had some good times, but it was really boring when the weather was miserable, which in her mind was pretty much most of the time. I said it sounded great fun and felt quite envious when I thought back to my own early childhood holiday memories. I kept the conversation focussed on Jennifer, but it was inevitable that she would eventually ask,

"What does your father do?"

I have been asked this question so many times, particularly by girls, that I have mastered a response that almost always guarantees at least a sympathetic, heavy petting session. But always before answering, I build up the atmosphere by allowing a long silent pause to descend as I model my face into its 'I'm trying to be brave' look. I can do this easily by thinking of my father, whom I only met twice, but those two brief moments had left me with an impression that has scarred my memory for life.

The first time was when I was about four years old, I had come down the stairs one morning to discover a strange man sitting in the kitchen, my mother, who was busy working over the stove, introduced us, "This is your father" she said in a very brusque voice without even turning from the stove. My father and I stared at each other in silence; there was an odd look in his eye, which I didn't at my young age understand. His hair was long and unkempt, and he had brought with him into the kitchen a new and unpleasant smell. After what seemed like an age, I simply turned on my heels and went back up the stairs to my room. When I returned later he was no longer there.

The second and final time I met my father was about three years later. As I was leaving for school one morning I collided with him as I ran out of our garden gate. He now sported a stained beard to go with his long greasy hair, but his style of dress and smell had not improved. As I stared into his eyes I again saw that look, a tired, hungry, despairing look, a look that reflected a life of disappointment, betrayal and injustice.

"Hello son", he rasped in a wheezing voice whilst attempting a smile that exposed the few remaining discoloured teeth in his mouth, "Is your mother in?" I never got the opportunity to reply as my mother's voice growled at full pitch from the kitchen door.

"Get yourself off to school before I take my stick to you" His eyes visibly twisted with pain before he raised his head and hobbled past me. He never looked back, and I never stopped looking. I never saw him again.

So, with these memories in my mind I gave her my well-rehearsed reply.

"He was an engineer in the Merchant Navy, he drowned when his ship sunk in a storm," I'd told this story so often that I had almost come to believe it myself. Jennifer immediately and sympathetically placed her hand on my arm and quietly whispered,

"I'm so sorry, he must have been a great loss to you."

"Not really," I replied, "I was very young, but it would have been great to have had a father when I was growing up." I tried to squeeze a tear out of the corner of my eye for further dramatic effect but failed. Jennifer's hand went to my shoulder to demonstrate her increasing sympathy.

"Did your mother not remarry?" Jennifer asked, unsure where to go with the conversation but obviously curious to find out more about my upbringing. Her question almost made me burst out with laughter as I tried to visualise what sort of lunatic would want to marry my mother, the only mental image that came to mind was that of my father standing at the garden gate.

"No, he had been the love of her life and she never looked at another man, she would often speak of him and tell me about some of his heroic adventures and sing some of the sea shanties he had taught her." I was struggling to contain my laughter and continue with this conversation; it surprised even me where this crap was coming from. Jennifer misunderstood my struggles as efforts to hold back my emotions, and with a single tear running down her face, her hand now caressing my neck, asked in a quivering voice.

"That's so sad, it must have been very difficult for both you and your mother, do you still live with her?" My evil alter ego was almost singing a sea shanty himself and was screaming encouragement in my head "Go on, tell her, you'll be in her knickers by sundown." I sat silently for a moment to gain a greater dramatic effect before simply explaining.

"She died when I was twelve in a climbing accident."

Jennifer sobbed, tears flowed down her face and her head lent onto my shoulder, her arm across my chest and cried,

"My god, you poor man". My mind lurched between different thoughts, from the right "For fucks sake, is this girl gullible or what?" and from the left "She's so sweet and gentle, I think I love her!"

Our conversation suddenly had to take on a more practical theme as we started to weave amongst the traffic on the South Circular Road, now in the throes of the rush hour. The traffic thinned as we joined the A4 and very soon we were entering the modern conurbation of Slough and Jennifer was able to give me directions to her parent's house, where she still lived. Finally, I turned the final corner into Sycamore Close, a collection of post war bungalows, each with its neatly tended gardens, fences and gates, all with freshly painted woodwork, everything obviously regularly and lovingly tended by each householder. It was hard to find anything out of place here, but it was instantly apparent that there was very little that could make you want to live there.

Parking outside, I helped Jennifer from the car, her foot and ankle were now very swollen, and she depended entirely on my support to reach the front door, which opened abruptly as my hand was reaching up with Jennifer's keys to open it. And there she was, my first sight of Jennifer's mother, Edith. Not a large woman either in height or girth, but she seemed to occupy more 'space' than her physical attributes should have generated. Her aura dominated everything within the limits of her sight and when she looked at you, you knew you were being looked at. She was smartly dressed, albeit in rather dated tweed 'Twin set' with the mandatory pearl necklace. Her glasses, brown plastic 'tortoiseshell' frames, with lenses that magnified her cruel eyes, rested firmly on her nose, a long and pointy appendage ideally suited to shade her small tight-lipped mouth. I could immediately sense that she had within her heart, the same warmth, love and joy that my own mother had had.

She seemed to glower at us both at the same time and when she demanded. "What's going on"? in a voice that was devoid of concern or sympathy, I felt Jennifer tense before she explained.

"I fell down and hurt my foot and ankle, Phillip has given me a lift home." There was no sign of this unpleasant woman relinquishing her domination of the front door opening until she was fully acquainted with all the facts.

"And who is Phillip and where is that other boy, Anthony?" she demanded.

59

"Anthony and I'd had an argument and he left me alone, Phillip acted as a Good Samaritan and has brought me home." Jennifer explained. "Can we come in, I promised Phillip that he could stay for supper?"

"I've told you before, I don't let strange people into my house, it was you that allowed that other boy in, against my wishes, and look at the state of you now, having to depend on another malingerer to lift you out of the gutter. It's really not good enough, where will it all end." She finished in a breathless rush to emphasise her exasperation.

My immediate reaction was to punch this bitch in the mouth and was about to release Jennifer when a weary voice from behind politely, but firmly asked.

"Edith, would you please stand aside and let us all in, I think we need a drink." Jennifer's Father had approached from the street whilst our attention had been distracted and he moved to Jennifer's other side to help her into the house, Edith was apparently not to be moved swiftly and continued to stare at us angrily, but obviously realising the futility of further confrontation, suddenly turned and stormed off into the dim interior of the house.

Jennifer introduced me to her father, George, and after we settled her onto the sofa he set off to pour some drinks. It was only then that I sat down and took in some of my surroundings; surroundings that I could only describe as bland and plain in a 'modern', drab kind of way, but it was the smell that captured my attention. There was a smell of beeswax and the smell of unpleasant cooking, but there was also a hint of that mysterious smell from my childhood, a musty smell that had lived with me in my mother's house and in the presbytery, a smell that shouldn't have existed in this relatively modern, well-furnished house in Slough. I just wanted to leave.

George returned with three glasses of sherry and handed them around, Edith being distinctive by her absence, which I felt to be a small consolation. Whilst we sipped our drinks, I would have preferred anything other sherry but felt it would be rude to ask for something else, George asked Jennifer to repeat to him the events that had resulted in her injuries. She told him of her argument with Anthony, omitting to disclose the reason, her painful stumble and again referred to me as a Good Samaritan. George turned to me and for the first time since our meeting, I saw into his eyes. Despite his warm smiling face the look in his eyes immediately confused me; a fatigued, dispirited, defeated and lonely look that I had first encountered when I met my own father for the first time. I couldn't stop the sorrow I felt for this man as he shook my hand, thanking me profusely and insisting that I stay for supper.

"We are all set for four as we expected Anthony to be eating with us". I thanked him and was further encourage by Jennifer as she took my hand and squeezed it reassuringly.

"But I don't think Jennifer's mother would be very pleased, so I think I'd better leave."

"It's too late for that, my boy, she's about to serve, so help Jennifer through to the table and I'll organise us some wine." George directed, as he collected our sherry glasses and left.

I helped Jennifer through to the dining room and was helping her into a chair when Edith entered the room, a sour look on her face, and with a furious glare in my direction she placed, non-too gently, on the table her Monday night speciality – Shepherd's Pie.

I should have just left there and then, and I often wonder how my life would have been if I had done, but I was still lusting after Jennifer's curves and I didn't want to offend George who had shown me nothing but kindness and appreciation. Throughout the evening I saw very little of Edith, she had served the meal, at first I believed she was being very generous as she heaped my plate with an extra spoonful, after the first mouthful, however, I realised that this was not a generous act at all. We ate in silence, each of us laboured through this watery, grey and gloopy mass. I tried particularly hard to clear my plate, smiling between each mouthful and making every effort to avoid any more of Edith's wrath. She had an uncanny skill at being able to observe everyone and everything around her, whilst at the same time allowing her busy, tight, blue lipped mouth, which was efficiently aided by her pink, flickering tongue, to make quick work of her portion of shepherd's pie. As soon as she finished she immediately returned to the kitchen without any ceremony. I felt sure the temperature of the room rose by 10 degrees!

When Jennifer announced that her foot was hurting and was going to bed, I thanked them and made to leave, but George asked me to stay and have a whisky "for the road". He went to help Jennifer up the stairs, leaving me alone, although not for one moment did I feel alone as I sensed I was being watched. I understood Anthony's dislike of Edith and agreed with his description of her as "an evil, rude bitch" and the "eating from her cauldron" was very apt.

George returned with two large glasses of whiskey and a packet of cigarettes. We proceeded to enjoy both whilst I learnt more about him. He told me that he was a partner in an insurance brokerage firm in London, he also told me, after I explained my own current occupation, that they were recruiting new staff and I should apply, the money would certainly be considerably more and the prospects for advancement within the firm were excellent. He wrote down the details of who to contact and gave me his card. He also gave me a little note from Jennifer that had been carefully and precisely written, thanking me for my help and asking if we could see each other again, she had added her telephone number and as I drove home I decided to call her and arrange a date. I felt very pleased with myself; I had got a new girlfriend, a 'Father figure' who I had instantly respected and admired and the likelihood of a new and prosperous career.

CHAPTER 7

Making a date with Jennifer proved to be quite difficult, however. I rang her several times, the phone was always, unfortunately, answered by the witch herself, Edith, and on recognising my voice she would always growl that Jennifer wasn't in and hang up. The only time I managed to ask if she could give her a message she told me in no uncertain terms that she wasn't a secretary and again hung up. What a bitch, but her attitude made me more determined to succeed and so I set off from Brighton early on Saturday morning and waited in the car outside the house until George came out and started pottering in the garden. He smiled welcomingly as I approached and as we shook hands I asked if Jennifer was at home.

"Of course, come in and I'll tell her you're here" he replied.

And so our courtship commenced, despite every obstacle possible being placed in my path by Edith. I grew to really hate this woman. Jennifer offered simple pleasures; her conversation and company was pleasant, but uninspiring, and the sex was nice, but unimaginative and routine, despite my efforts to encourage her towards new levels of creativity.

My relationship with George developed; I applied and secured a very good job within his firm and after 6 months of training I had doubled my salary and secured a new dark blue Ford Escort with red upholstery, so much sportier than the ageing, sedentary car from my previous employment. I felt like the king of the road and loved the drive from Brighton to work or to Jennifer's on the A23; on some of the dual carriageway sections I hit speeds of over 90 mph.

During these journeys, I always marvelled at how the cars I had driven had improved over the years, from my first car, a very decrepit, blue Ford Anglia, identical in many ways to The Weasley's Ford Anglia in the Harry Potter movie, the only difference, obviously, was its lack of magical powers and an ability to fly. I often reflected on how this car had come to a very sad end.

I was only 17 and had only had my driving licence for a few months before I used all my savings to procure this vehicle. The freedom it gave me to take trips out to the countryside at the weekends and to drive my friends home from college, increased my popularity dramatically. In no time I rarely drove the car alone and usually had a pretty girl in the passenger seat, or occasionally in the back seat if my luck was in!

One girl that I was particularly attracted to was Alice Robson, she was stunningly beautiful with long blond hair, blue eyes, the softest of lips and a cheerleader's figure. At first, I was besotted with Alice, we would talk and talk and talk, which at the beginning of a relationship is very important, but after months becomes irritating to a young guy who, despite his courteous, feigned interest in her endless conversation, only wanted to grope her body or better still, to 'screw the pants off her'. Alice, despite my efforts; I spent all my money on buying her little gifts, treating her to the cinema, including fish suppers, we shared burger meals, picnics, local dances, I tried everything in the hope that my hand be allowed to slide over one of her breasts, but no, she wanted to 'save herself'.

For me our relationship began to decline during one of our 'wrestling matches' in the back of my car one Saturday night. We had driven to and parked on the side of small track that was off the main road and led eventually down to a disused quarry. It was secluded and only occasionally frequented by other lovers or passers-by. Suddenly Alice broke away from our embrace, straightened her hair, moved into the front seat and began talking about her real dream for our relationship. She could clearly see us getting married and she went on and on about the dress and the hundreds of people that would come to wedding and adore her. She could clearly see the architectural designed house that she would live in and she described in detail her bedroom, all decked out with nauseatingly pink everything. Her husband was only there to adore her, apparently she never wanted to have sex and would fulfil her incredible motherly skills by adopting orphans that she would love and cherish.

I was very frustrated and became increasingly angry as I came to realise that, even if I was to marry her, buy her a house and spend my life telling her how wonderful she was, I was still unlikely ever to have sex with her. She wanted to be a 'Virgin Mother' and her husband had to be a simple eunuch. I wished I'd had this discussion with her a few months earlier, I wouldn't have wasted all my money and efforts trying to develop a more intimate relationship. She finally stopped talking and we sat in silence for a few minutes before I got out of the car and sat on the bonnet and continued to fume over a cigarette. Alice just sat in the car. I continued to smoke one cigarette after the other. Our 'standoff' was finally relieved when she wound the window down to say that she was ready to go home now.

I wanted to frighten her or at least inflict some small, petulant rebuke for her selfish frigidity, so when I got behind the wheel I deliberately attempted to start the car without pulling the choke out, a procedure that I knew would result in the car failing to start. After only a few attempts the battery began to fail, and the engine only turned very slowly with a last groaning effort.

"That's it" I said, "you'll have to get out and push the car."

"I'm not getting out of the car," snorted Alice indignantly "it's dark and creepy out there."

"The only way we're going to get the car going is with a bump start, and that requires someone giving it a push and as there is nobody else around, it means you'll have to push it or stay in the car all night."

"Why don't you push it," Alice demanded angrily, "I'm not getting out of the car and I certainly don't intend spending the night here."

"The reason I can't push it is that it requires someone to sit behind the wheel and let the clutch out when the car gets moving, then to use the throttle to keep the engine going when it starts. As you can't drive, it means that I will be sitting behind the wheel while you're pushing." My plan was simple in that I intended to drive off down the track after the car had started and leave her in the dark, I would then wait a minute or two before driving back to pick her up. A small token of justice to satisfy my frustrated anger.

"It cannot be difficult," she stubbornly continued, "just show me what to do and then you can push the car."

A long, angry silence settled in the car once more, and as we glared at each other I realised that I had little choice but to agree. I showed her how she had to have the ignition on, the clutch depressed, the gear engaged in second and how she must release the clutch when I had got the car moving sufficiently fast. I told her to use the throttle to give it a few revs when it did start and then to re-engage the clutch and stop so I could take over. I had to explain all of this twice before she confirmed, quite dismissively, that it was all very straightforward, and she could manage.

I climbed out of the car and told her to release the hand brake and to get ready. The car was resting in a slight hollow and I had to rock the car to get it over the hump, and with one final push the car began its forward motion. I pushed and the car quickly began to pick up sufficient speed, so I shouted

"Release the clutch"

Continuing to follow the car at a jogging pace, I watched as it started its kangaroo coughing motion as the momentum turned over the engine and it attempted to start. Suddenly it roared into life and accelerated away.

"Use the brakes," I shouted, now running flat out to keep up. The car continued to accelerate forward, the engine beginning to scream with effort.

"Use the fucking brakes," I shouted again. Still running as fast as I could, I watched the car as it weaved erratically down the track before suddenly veering off to the right and plunging through the dense ferns. The car continued to accelerate, and the engine squealed even louder, now accompanied with the sound of the suspension as it 'thwumped' over the potholes and grassy tufts. I ran and slipped through the undergrowth but quickly lost sight of the car in the darkness and could only follow the sounds of the 'thwumping' and the screaming of the engine.

The noise suddenly stopped and the engine note changed. It was like the car was going into a tunnel, the sound disappearing into the distance. This sound also abruptly ended with an almighty crash followed by loud 'Woof!' and everything was suddenly revealed, a yellow glow appeared some distance in front of me. I could see the track through the undergrowth where the car had ploughed through, and I could see where it ended and the yellow glow of nothingness started. My pace slowed as I approached the edge of the old quarry face and on looking down I could see the crumbled remains of my car shrouded with smoke and flames.

I was frozen to the spot, I couldn't believe what had happened, I just stood there watching the flames slowly diminish and the darkness progressively return. I didn't know what to do and as my senses began to return I realised I'd left my cigarettes in the car.

CHAPTER 8

The rest of that night and the following day were a bit of a blur. The walk through the darkness to find a house and have the old couple who lived there summon help. The arrival of the police, ambulance and fire engine and me having to guide this procession of blue flashing lights to the scene of the accident. My journey to the police station, all the questions, which I struggled to answer, all I could say and constantly repeat was. "She drove off the edge of the cliff"

Sometime the following day, after fitfully sleeping in a cell, I was once again asked to describe exactly what had happened. This time, and feeling much calmer, I was able to describe in detail the events that had led to the accident. Everything was written down and read back to me and I signed the statement. I thought that would be it, but no, the police sergeant had other ideas.

"Your girlfriend died last night in a horrible and terrifying way. You have described a rather implausible story as to how this 'accident' happened, but do you know what son, I don't believe a word of it. I think when she refused to have sex, you killed her and then orchestrated this 'accident' to cover up your crime. I think when we finish the autopsy report and we analyse the evidence on the ground, we will discover that your apparent 'accident' is nothing but a pack of lies. It would be much easier on you if you just told me the truth now. I can still let you change your statement before we go any further"

"I have told you the truth, I couldn't have killed Alice, I loved her" I replied as convincingly as I could.

My foster parents, schoolteachers and friends supported my claim of innocence, insisting that I was not capable of such a crime. The autopsy revealed very little other than that the remains of Alice's body had suffered severe trauma in the crash and had been burnt almost to a skeleton. The coroner recorded an accidental death and that ended my affair with Alice.

CHAPTER 9

My attention returned to the drive towards London on the A23, my memories of Alice bringing a wry smile to my face, I even chuckled as I realised that her lifetime ambition to be a 'Virgin Mother', had at least been partially achieved on her death, she'd only failed to become a 'Mother'!

CHAPTER 10

George had become like a father figure. He was kind and gentle, supportive and always offered help, support and advice whenever I needed it. I decided that rather than living in Brighton I should move closer to my work, George and of course Jennifer. I think this was the time that my life became set and 'The Routine' started. I firstly made the mistake of moving into a flat in Slough. Secondly, and more out of obligation and respect for George, I proposed to Jennifer. The wedding was planned and organised with a zealous, passionless fervour by the dragon herself, Edith. Everything was to be done her way, her church, her choice of flowers, her choice of attire for the wedding party, her choice of venue for the reception, her choice of menu and most importantly, who was invited. She dominated everyone and everything until in a moment of extreme awkwardness, pushed even the mild-mannered George to raising his voice in objection, a short-lived rebellion that Edith quickly crushed with cruel disregard.

The wedding planning went on for over 9 months and I watched almost daily as the light in

George's eyes slowly faded and his energy for life began to disappear, a look of frustration, dispirited disappointment and disillusionment took over his very being. I was constantly reminded of that figure with the haunted eyes standing at the garden gate from my childhood memory.

Finally, the ordeal was over, the wedding day and our honeymoon in Bognor Regis was parked into that little corner of your mind reserved for events not to be repeated. Only two things remain to this day as a constant reminder. The first is the white plastic presentation folder of photographs that rest on the bookshelf in the sitting room, a standing testament, like some monument to a mindless period of my life. The second is one of my few fond memories from that time; it was the evening of the wedding rehearsal, a tiring and repetitive ordeal that had even exhausted the vicar. Tired and irritable we had left the church, I opened the car door, most politely I thought, to let Edith climb in, and whether I was a little hasty or Edith was a little slow I cannot be sure, but I slammed the heavy car door, crushing and trapping her fingers. Such a fond memory; her face twisted into a grimace of pain, her small blue lips parted as her screams wailed from inside the car. I felt such instant joy, a joy that I believe both George and Jennifer shared as none of us moved, enjoying this shrieking banshee, writhing in agony in front of our eyes. Unfortunately, all good things had to come to an end and as my inaction bordered on the point of being rude, I reopened the door. Thank God, things were even worse than I could have hoped for, at least two of her fingers were definitely crushed and broken, as could be clearly seen from the almost right angular and backward direction they had unnaturally achieved. But her language, bloody hell! vile didn't do it justice, it was spectacular and full of expletives that even a drunken navvy would have struggled to express after zipping his penis into the fly of his trousers, and they were all directed at me. Her hat fell from her head onto the ground as she danced around like a rabid marionette; it was crushed underfoot in my rather laboured efforts to help. Oh, happy days, I still feel a warm satisfaction rise from my stomach as I think of this moment and even on those occasions when Jennifer would take out the photo album, the images of Edith with her hand plastered and in a sling, has fortified me ever since.

Those bleak Sunday afternoons when Jennifer would take out 'The Album' to show to the children or friends, she would also bring out several of the other photo albums to illustrate all the other happy occasions in our life together. Photos of our children growing up, their evolution from being ugly screaming babies, to brats, to teenage savages, to their current mature state of adulthood and their thoughtless, selfish, greedy mannerisms. Photos of our annual holidays to Devon, every year the same; same caravan, same view, same caravan friends, same chip shop. None of the fleshy hotspots of Ibitha or the romance of Italy or the culinary delights of France for us, no, Jennifer didn't like the heat or all 'those foreigners'. Photographs of our house in Slough that we'd bought in the second year of marriage, some of these photographs had now become a little grainy with age, but by retaking the same picture today it could easily be replaced, as the image had hardly changed, incredibly even the plants in the garden had seemed to resist change under Jennifer's careful management.

The photo albums recorded our lives for what they were, and still are; routine, unimaginative, uncreative and unfulfilling. Boring.

CHAPTER 11

My relationship with George became closer and closer, we always travelled to work together and with his support and guidance he helped me progress to a senior position within the firm. We went to sporting events together; his favourite was cricket and since he was a member we often went to The Oval cricket ground to watch Surrey or occasionally a Test Match. He knew I wasn't too enthusiastic about cricket and so he would let me take him to the Rugby Internationals when they were played at Twickenham. We enjoyed each other's company and my feelings for him grew to genuine admiration and love.

As the years moved on it broke my heart as I watch this kind and gentle man's health and spirit decline; remarkably I seemed to be the only one who noticed or cared. Jennifer just laughed when I drew her attention to it, she commented with disinterest.

"Age affects us all and remember he's in his sixties now, so he's no spring chicken."

I asked George several times if he was all right and he would simply shrug his shoulders and reply.

"I'm fine, little things in life wear you down, but that's just the way it is." He always ended this reassurance with the smile of a martyr that told me everything about "the little things of life".

Edith was not someone you could discuss any form of illness with, she always dismissed any health-related complaints as "the weaknesses of malingerers and the working classes". So, when I went around one evening after work to enquire into George's well-being; he most unusually hadn't been to the office that day, I was briskly dismissed from the doorstep by Edith, her pink tongue swiping angrily across her blue lips as she stated crossly.

"He only has a sniffle and stop fussing over him, it's very irritating." The end of the sentence was a little muffled as the door closed firmly to illustrate that no further foolish discussion was welcome, and certainly not with me.

I never saw George again as two days later he died. His death certificate stated that he died of cancer, but no matter what the medical diagnoses was, I knew he had died from lack of love and care. He died of a heart broken by all those sad emotions that had shone from his eyes. It left me very upset and dejected.

CHAPTER 12

It was the robustness of Jennifer and Edith that raised me from this malaise of sadness, they quickly turned events around to ensure my feelings changed to bitterness and anger. George's death, and apparently his entire existence seemed to be quickly forgotten; even before the funeral his clothes and belongings were being put into boxes and black bin bags ready for their passage to the jumble sale and bric-a-brac charity shops. They were ruthless in their efforts to return to the security of their 'normal' routines and that nothing in their life would be affected by the inconvenience that George had caused.

Everything did indeed quickly return to 'normal', but with one very unfortunate and particularly unwelcome change, Jennifer began to care for her mother. She would explain her newly adopted role by constantly reminding me, and the children, and anyone who enquired, "Well, she's a widow now and we have a duty to care for her." At first, I thought she was simply fulfilling a traditional obligation, but as she began to spend more and more time with Edith, she began to learn many of her dark skills; the principal being the art of 'how to make everyone's life a misery'. She began to gain more and more of Edith's cookery talents and they spent hours together, practicing recipes and working out the most efficient ways to ruin good food. She began to learn many of her talents for rudeness, she even began to emulate many of her mannerisms, I could swear that Jennifer's mouth began to shrink, her lips took on a bluish tinge and her tongue became pinker. Over time Jennifer was slowly becoming Edith.

CHAPTER 13

Diary note:

Thursday morning, felt nauseous all night, the 'macaroni and cheese bake', our usual Wednesday night supper, had lain heavy in my stomach and the pervading smell of the jumble sale boxes and contents had kept bringing back those horrible memories. It's my birthday today, not that it's important to anyone, my birth date has long since been forgotten by everyone, not that they ever made it a cause for celebration, even in those distant days when they did remember it. The last present I received from Edith was a second-hand tool kit that she'd brought home from the church bazaar; she thought it would encourage me to at least try at some small DIY jobs around the house. The thought of picking up a hammer and doing anything other than sinking it into her skull seemed ridiculous and the tools were quickly retired to the garage.

Perhaps soon I may find a use for them after all.

I also feel a bit depressed again today, I usually do when it's my birthday, but it's every time I stand in front of the mirror shaving in the morning, and this morning is the worst. The reflection of my eyes tells of a life that has followed a path trodden by too many bitter moments. I try to remember when it was that I first saw in my own eyes the same level of misery that lived in my father's and George's eyes, I think it was probably that Monday after George's funeral when Jennifer served me Shepherd's Pie, and nothing had changed. I'm determined to make this 'look' disappear as soon as possible, my thoughts are slowly developing, and I have decided to carefully plan three possible options for consideration, selection and refinement to achieve my goal. A foolish person would rush this process, and whilst I feel a growing urgency, I must remember the teachings in the Personal Development Training Course – the 5 'Ps' - "Purpose,

Patience, Planning, Perseverance and Performance".

Off to work, I've no appointments so I can focus on 'The Planning' element of my 'Project'.

Diary note:

Thursday – on train going home.

Quiet day at the office, as expected. Feeling very positive and excited as I have begun to develop some plans of how to kill Jennifer, and the possible consequences. I have three ideas now, which all need a great deal of thought and investigation; I will start making notes and expanding them tomorrow. Veronica didn't have any tights on today, which seemed a little improper, but it did feel like a bit of a birthday treat. No point in wondering what's for dinner tonight, it's Thursday, so it will be 'toad in the hole' cooked to a level of dryness that no quantity of the accompanying liquid that Jennifer offers as gravy can sate. I always soldier through this ordeal because it's then rice pudding for desert, which is delicious, I'm certain it must come from a tin, but I can't be sure, it's my favourite course of the week, so credit where credit's due, I try to be balanced in my critical judgments.

CHAPTER 14

Plan 1 – 'The Household Accident'.

This plan is an obvious one for me to follow, being an insurance specialist, I know that a great many accidents and injuries occur in the home. Accidents in the bathroom, falling down stairs, falling through glass doors, electrocution and then the most popular, scalding, burning, poisoning, choking, cutting/stabbing with knives and fire. My difficulties with orchestrating an 'accident' in the home, is trying to arrange it in such a way that it results in certain death and with no suggestion of my involvement. I have, over the years, watched many police programmes and gained a level of understanding, at least equal to the average man, of forensics. No matter how Jennifer dies I will be a suspect until they conclude otherwise, therefore I cannot do anything that is beyond my own level of skills, like my dream of rigging a gas explosion. Shame, I still enjoy those images.

After a process of thought and elimination, I visualise a plan to kill Jennifer in the bathroom. In this room, several 'accidents' are possible. Drowning and slipping on wet surfaces are obvious, but not so obvious are electrocution, drinking bleach and other chemicals, and hanging. Finding the last two on the list quite difficult to imagine how they could occur under any circumstances, I focus on the more obvious.

Having watched the movie "Groundhog Day" I have seen the effects on a person when a toaster is dropped in the bath, and coincidentally, Jennifer often listens to her radio, which she plugs into the shaver socket. This would seem like an opportunity worth investigating, it would be so simple and easy and the thought of her twitching and writhing around in the bath enjoying the effects of 240 volts passing through her, is very encouraging. I need to test this plan.

CHAPTER 15

Diary note:

Saturday morning. Had to get up early this morning to help Jennifer, but it was a real pleasure getting the car loaded with the last of the jumble sale boxes before waving goodbye to her as she left for the whole day, what a treat. I have planned out my day and I have six things to do: -

1) Take the limp, unappetising, cellophane wrapped cheese sandwich that Jennifer has prepared for my lunch and put it in the first rubbish bin I find.

2) Go to Greggs the Bakers and buy two of their large, greasy sausage rolls with that delicious pink' meat' filling, I love these, full of taste and flavour and with a packet of smoky bacon crisps and a couple of bottles of beer, I will look forward to an enjoyable lunch in front of the television watching England against Scotland in a Six Nations Rugby match. A little secret habit that George and I established over the years before his death.

3) Go to the supermarket and buy a cheap hair dryer.

4) Go to the pet shop and buy a guinea pig. I need a 'guinea pig' for my experiment.

5) Carry out the planned experiment and dispose of the evidence.

6) Watch the rugby.

A fun and interesting Saturday that I'm looking forward to.

I was quite pleased in a strange sort of way with my morning's efforts, although not everything had gone entirely to plan. I had finally managed to get everything bought, the guinea pig had to be a hamster, whose name was Joey, which somehow made the whole experiment feel a little personal. When I'd gone to the pet shop the owner informed me that he didn't have any guinea pigs left, but had some more coming in for the following weekend. I explained that it was to be a present for my grandson's birthday the following day and I had forgotten to organise the gift I had promised him, he was so looking forward to having a little pet of his own. The owner was most sympathetic and explained that the only little pet he had that wasn't reserved was a hamster that a little girl and her mother had brought in on the Friday afternoon because her brother had developed an allergy to the dust and fur of the animal. The owner further explained that the mother had only asked that it go to a 'good home' and that a donation be made to the RSPCA, he rattled the collection box on the counter for emphasis. So, £20 into the box, £15 for a little cage, £5 for some food and I walked out of the shop with a hamster that had been named Joey by the little girl.

When it came to the 'experiment' however, I found it quite difficult; Joey was actually very cute with his big circular eyes that melted your heart, he seemed to gaze affectionately and trustingly at you as he munched happily on a piece of celery I had taken from the fridge for him. I wished I'd had a little pet called Joey when I'd been young.

Unfortunately however, cute or not, his life's purpose as a child's pet was at an end and he was about to embark on a new career as a 'guinea pig'.

As I tipped him into the bath water, which I had thoughtfully filled with warm water so he wouldn't get a chill, his little legs worked like pistons as they propelled him around the water line of the bath. I hadn't realised what good swimmers hamsters were, and I enjoyed watching and playing with him as he swam backwards and forwards, squeaking with apparent joy.

With the hairdryer plugged in and switched on, I nervously stood holding it at arms length above the water. After a final minute of consideration for my own safety, I released the whirring appliance and it hit the water with a sizzling splash.

What happened next was not the outcome I'd visualised and expected. As I released the hair dryer, I quickly stepped back to avoid being close to the expected sparks and smoke, but the instant it hit the water the lights went out and I was plunged into darkness. Thinking that someone had turned them off I spun around, trying to work out a suitable explanation for this rather bizarre scene in the bathroom, but between stepping back, spinning around, the sudden darkness, I stumbled and fell backwards thumping my head off the side of the sink before hitting the floor.

As I began to recover, feeling quite dizzy and rubbing at the pain at the back of my head that was already growing into a sizeable lump, I realised what had happened. The trip switch had knocked the electricity off. I felt a little relieved that someone hadn't actually caught me in the act of some strange animal torture, however, I was also very annoyed; how fucking stupid can you be, it was obvious that would happen now I thought about it, they obviously didn't have trip switches in the Groundhog Day hotel. Pulling myself up, I gingerly fumbled along the wall to the door, I opened it to let in some light before returning to the bath, in the gloom I could see the hair dryer languishing uselessly under the still surface of the water, its coiled cable trailing up the side and over the edge of the bath to the shaver socket. What was missing from this tranquil picture was Joey, he'd obviously had enough swimming around and made his exit by climbing the cable. I searched everywhere, but the little fella had disappeared.

Having restored the electricity and tidied everything away, I once again continued to search for Joey, softly calling his name, as I looked under every bed, amongst the piles of towels and clothes, in every cupboard and wardrobe, before finally having to accept that he had really disappeared and was not in the house. Furious with my complete incompetence and realising that time had moved on, and the rugby kick off was in twenty minutes, I rushed to the kitchen, warmed up the sausage rolls, opened a bottle of beer, piled the crisps onto a plate, turned on the television to be greeted by the anthems, which I began singing along to, firstly "Flower of Scotland" , so much cheerier that than the English "God Save Our Gracious Queen", but I gave each my best effort.

Having consumed my lunch, drank my beers, conducted another quick search for Joey during the half time break, I sat back in the chair, hoping that the second half was better than the drab and uninspiring first. I hated all the numerous new rules; the game seemed to have become sterile and an almost 'contact free' sport, all in the interests of 'Health and Safety'. No more did you have the scraps and punch ups in the Rucks and Scrums that were forever happening in the days when I played rugby at school.

The boredom of the match and the influence of the beers had me drifting in a light slumber and I recalled those wonderful schoolboy rugby matches. One particular match floated across my mind. I remembered it was a very cold day as we ran onto the pitch; the ground was still frozen from the overnight frost. We all limbered up trying to warm ourselves and soon there was a light mist floating across the field as our breath blew out of our mouths like factory chimneys. The game kicked off and in no time our knees and elbows were grazed from the repeated contact with the hard, rough ground, but we didn't mind because by the end of the first half we were winning 18 – 3, a score that was largely due to our winger, Paul Anderson.

I hated Paul fucking Anderson, he had everything; the speed of a greyhound, long sturdy legs and body that possessed an agility that allowed him to avoid most tackles and out-sprint all the opposition. His commanding presence made him a popular choice for captain with his teammates. His blond hair, blue eyes, handsome looks and athletic prowess also made him very popular with the girls, they worshipped and adored him, blushing and giggling every time he walked by them. To make matters even worse, his academic abilities were on par with his physical perfection and he was highly thought of by all the teachers and the Headmaster himself, who had made him a junior prefect at the beginning of term.

As a Prefect, Mr Perfect Paul fucking Anderson had quickly let this newly awarded power go straight to his head. He chose those individual that he didn't like or weren't his friend or couldn't give him things he wanted, to pick on, reporting them to the teacher or even on occasions the Headmaster, for every minor offence or even sometimes fictitious offences. As I didn't fall into any category to receive favourable treatment from him, I was threatened, bullied and persecuted by him remorselessly. He reminded me constantly that I didn't have any real parents and he nicknamed me "The Orphan". Often when the rugby team selection was put up on the school notice board, my position at No. 8, was simply listed as 'Orphan' as opposed to my surname. I detested this school idol, but felt powerless to do anything about it, that was until the second half of the rugby match played that day on the frozen surface of the school field.

Paul was running amok, two more converted tries taking the score to 32 – 3, had the opposition in tatters. We were again on the attack and Paul had once again caught the ball and embarked on another sprint up the field with the rest of us trying to keep pace in support. Paul didn't however escape the opposing teams tackles this time and he was brought down, falling heavily. All the forward players, myself included, piled in, anxious to secure the ball, and here lies the great difference between the modern game of rugby and the style of rugby of my youth. Now, as the ball fails to be released quickly the referee blows his whistle and stops the game, back then it continued as a bruising and lengthy battle on the ground that either resulted in a punch up or the ball being secured by one of the teams, allowing the game to continue.

We pushed and shoved, wrestled and shouted at each other, I was in the thick of it and was pushing with all my might, having secured a warm soft spot on the ground with my knee which was giving excellent leverage for my efforts. As the 'ruck' began to move forwards I looked down to discover that the 'warm spot' from which my knee had been finding such a good grip, was in fact Paul Anderson's throat. His face had already turned a rather blue colour and his bulging eyes looked back at me pleadingly, I could see that he was regretting all the psychological pain he had inflicted on me, but I couldn't, at that moment, accept his regrets or an apology even, if he could have vocalised one, which obviously he couldn't, so I pressed down harder with my knee, enjoying the look of understanding and acceptance that crossed his contorted face, we glared at each other before his eyes glazed over as his life finally disappeared.

The ball finally escaped the writhing heap of bodies into our possession and we were all quickly up and running towards the opposition goal line, I was rewarded for all my efforts by being passed the ball and scoring another try, right under the posts. What an exhilarating few moments. We all cheered as we made our way back to the halfway line to restart the game, well fourteen of us did, Paul Anderson remained prostrate on the ground.

What a terrible accident, and what a great disappointment that the game had to be abandoned when we were winning by such a large margin.

My focus returned to the rather stop start process of the modern game, realising that accidents like the one involving Mr Perfect Paul Fucking Anderson, Prefect, Team Captain and All-Round Jolly Good Fellow, could not be allowed to happen again, but I still felt this

England v Scotland match could've been more interesting to watch with the addition of some real physical action.

The game over, I resumed once again my search for the elusive Joey, but after a further forty minutes I gave up, deciding that he had either escaped from the house somehow or had found some secret place within the house that was warm and comfortable. I would keep a careful watch and if he did make an appearance, I could give him some more of his favourite treats before returning him to the pet shop.

Unfortunately for Joey this was not going to happen. Jennifer returned at 6.30, the Jumble Sale had not been a success and she seemed to have more boxes of junk than she had when she left, but she returned having done something that she hadn't done in years, she brought home two fish suppers from the chip shop, what a wonderful women, I nearly forgave her for all the years of Saturday night misery eating the rubbery omelette and limp salad that was our usual fare. The only exception to this menu was when we would be invited to a friend's house or have friends around for dinner. Fortunately, this was a very rare occasion, I think I preferred the omelette.

I say 'friends', but they weren't really friends, we've never known anyone that we would call a true friend. They were always acquaintances of Jennifer, people she knew from the church or the charity shop or Meals on Wheels. I remember our last 'soiree', there were six of us including Jennifer and me. The vicar was there, the vicar was always there; a tall, pompous preacher, who did little but lecture to anyone who would either listen or had no choice but to listen. You could never have a conversation with him on any topic, without him giving a Godly answer by quoting Parables or Scriptures. He believed there was an answer to every single problem or crisis that occurred in life written in the bible. To make things worse, he always gave his 'mini sermons' with an arrogant 'know it all' smirk and the nodding of his head. There was no arguing with him, he was always right, or so he and his 'flock' believed. I just avoided talking to him and whenever he came for supper I always ensured he sat next to Jennifer. The problem for me was that I may have separated myself from the vicar, but it meant I had to sit next to one of the other guests, which usually meant the vicar's wife, Angela.

Angela was the organiser and the true power behind the 'throne'. As the Vicar only had two duties in life, churchly sermons and boring the arse of everyone with his constant preaching and bible quotes, Angela did everything else; she ran the vicarage, cooking, cleaning, washing, ironing, even dressing the vicar, apparently. Fortunately, she was very efficient and managed to complete her daily chores by mid-morning every day, leaving her bounteous time to terrify and persecute all the female parishioners into performing their dutiful tasks. The slightest disagreement with her spoken command, would result in the ultimate community shame, that of being demoted from the more 'respectable' duties in the Church. These respectable duties included flowering arranging, polishing the silver on the alter, setting out the hymnals, being part of the choir or preparing and distributing the church newsletter. Demotion caused by a single word of dissent, would result in a poor unfortunate being reduced to tears as she was instructed to sweep and wash the floors or worse still, not be asked to do anything. This was all about social status and if you weren't asked to do anything, you would also be excluded from 'tea at the vicarage' where these absentees were subjected to 'character assassinations' as the 'blessed ones' viciously gossiped about their failings.

Jennifer, naturally would never invite any of those who were not in this top echelon of church society, that would have been another offence to Angela and the church. So, at our dinner party the other two guests were also ladies of this 'inner circle'; their husbands had obviously learnt from previous harsh experience, to avoid these soirees, their wives always explaining that, as they were so important, they found it difficult to find the time and had to attend meetings or conferences, usually as far away from Slough as possible. Sensible, I had pulled the same stunt on several occasions myself.

The first lady, Mrs Wilkinson, or Mary to her friends, so I called her Mrs Wilkinson, was a brute of a woman; furniture groaned as she approached to rest her enormous bulk. She constantly explained that she had a thyroid problem that caused her ever growing size, but when you watched as she fed 'at the trough', even at Jennifer's trough, I didn't believe the thyroid had much to do with the punishment she inflicted on even the most robust of chairs. She was however, very smart in her uniform of a cream blouse, pearl necklace, a tweed 'twinset', heavy duty stockings, that only just managed to contain her bulky 'tree trunk' legs, ending in the mandatory stout, brown, leather shoes. She was held in particularly high esteem by Angela as she was responsible for the choir, leading them in joyful harmony with her baritone voice. Her favourite topic of conversation, that I had no choice but to listen to, was the failure of modern, young mothers to discipline their children.

"Take a stick to them, that's what I say," she brayed, "all this liberal nonsense of caring talk and gentle persuasion to educate children will never work, we're just creating a society of hooligans and delinquents." I wondered what part of the bible she had learnt this from, I suspect she only really believed in God's abusive passions as taught in the Old Testament. Jesus was far too liberal

Our other guest, Mrs Sylvia Crisp, was the exact opposite to Mrs Wilkinson; A wraith of a woman whose skin just managed to stretch over her bones and tendons, thin blue veins made ink like lines across the backs of her hands, which I found amazing and couldn't stop looking at. Her sunken face had a skeletal quality to it and her colourless eyes seemed to bulge from their huge darkened sockets. She ate like a mouse, nibbling a little bit here and a little bit there, which seemed to exaggerate further the glutenous activities of Mrs Wilkinson. Mrs Crisp's redeeming feature was that she hardly ever spoke, so she could easily be ignored, her true vocation was her love of music and her ability to play the organ, it was a shame we didn't have one in the house, any distraction would've been welcomed.

The evening dragged along, nobody seemed to have much to say or were too fearful to say the wrong thing, which resulted in quite long periods of awkward silence around the table where everyone pretended to be enjoying their meal. To make the evening even more enjoyable, I had only been allowed to open one bottle of wine, which I had carefully shared amongst us all by pouring dribbles into each glass on several occasions, trying to give the impression of generosity, but without displaying any eagerness for the evils of drink. By the time our guests left, I had chronic heartburn and indigestion; the combination of Jennifer's culinary skills, the dreadful company, the stress of constantly trying to make conversation and the almost complete lack of alcohol had taken its toll on both my physical and mental health.

It was a relief to be wearing rubber gloves and washing the dishes, something constructive, while Jennifer cleared everything away. She had obviously been thinking about the evening as she suddenly announced.

"That was one of the best nights I've had in a long time, I really think everyone enjoyed themselves. Obviously, my menu selection was perfect as they all scraped their plates." I wondered which dinner party Jennifer had been to and I decided she was completely fucking deluded; it had been one of the worst nights of my life.

CHAPTER 16

Diary note:

Sunday morning. Having a lie in. Jennifer got up early to begin preparing lunch, she has invited all the family around again today "so we may enjoy some quality time with the grandchildren"- oh fucking joy!

I have been reflecting on yesterday's experiments and have concluded that electrocution is not an option, and as a woman like Jennifer doesn't get 'accidentally' strangled, stabbed, hung or struck by a blunt instrument, I ruled out these other possibilities. I also concluded that drugs or poisoning would be very difficult to explain, and from my list of initial options this only left being burnt to death, which I've already discounted, or drowning.

Drowning requires consideration. I could enter the bathroom while Jennifer was showering, hit her over the head with something that would have to emulate the curved shape of the roll top bath, then lay her unconscious body back into the bath and gently hold her head under water until she drowned. This sounded reasonably straightforward and very much like a real accident, it would be obvious to all that she had slipped in the shower knocking herself out and then drowned.

My thoughts and diary notes were abruptly interrupted by the sounds of shouting and banging from downstairs and my name being called in an urgent tone. Running downstairs, quickly pulling my dressing gown on, I rushed into the kitchen to see Jennifer standing like a formidable gladiator over the crushed and bloody remains of Joey.

"It's a fucking rat," snarled the red-faced combatant, her hand still brandishing a weighty meat tenderising mallet, something I didn't know we even had and something that, despite her apparent skill with the disposal of Joey, I'm sure she had never used in the preparation of any meat served from her kitchen.

"A rat?" I asked, knowing full well that it wasn't a rat, "how's that got in the house?"

"How would I know" glowered Jennifer, "but I've killed it, so you can clear up the mess."

"You must have brought it back with you from the jumble sale in one of the cardboard boxes," I stared back at her accusingly, "god knows what else is now back in our attic." Jennifer dropped the tenderiser into the sink and went back to her luncheon preparations without any further discussion, my explanation was obviously plausible and, as she believed that the arrival of the rodent may be her fault, the topic was immediately dropped, and nothing would ever be mentioned again.

Scraping Joey off the floor really saddened me; his little fluffy ears, his long spikey whiskers, his tiny 'nibbly' mouth and his large round black eyes, which were still very cute but were now frozen in a look of shocked surprise when his furry golden body had been crushed by several blows of the meat hammer that had been wielded, rather cruelly and unnecessarily I believed, by Jennifer. I carried him out to the garden, where I apologised once again, before burying him. Poor little bugger!

CHAPTER 17

Diary note:

On the train. Monday again! Yesterday was dreadful, between the unfortunate death of Joey and a tasteless lunch of string, fat and skin that apparently had existed at one time on the shoulders of a spring lamb. All in the company of the bloody family and the diabolical brats; who decided to exhume Joey and give him a full post-mortem, leaving entrails and carcass all over the lawn. I feel even more woeful than normal. On a positive note, I have now planned in detail 'The Bathroom Accident'. I believe that my mission has been helped by Jennifer herself and her lunch menu, as I know what the ideal murder weapon can be, a frozen leg of lamb, I remember this murder weapon being used in one of the Roald Dahl stories.

I imagine myself carrying this cold bludgeon up the stairs and along the landing towards the bathroom, the only sound being the spraying of the shower water. I cautiously approach the door, the debate raging in my head, "don't do it, you'll get caught" from one side and "go on, get in there and kill the bitch" from the other. I pause for only a moment before opening the door and peering in. I can see Jennifer's outline standing in the bath behind the shower curtain, her arms clearly raised as she washes her hair. I don't hesitate, quickly and silently I enter and move close, she remains completely unaware of my presence. I flex my arm, feeling the weight of the weapon before raising it like a baseball bat and swinging it forward with some force, travelling directly towards the back of Jennifer's head. The shower curtain offers no resistance, but as it meets its target the momentum slows before stopping abruptly as her face is driven forward into the tiled wall in front of her. I pull back the joint preparing to hit her again if necessary, but she crumples like a stone into the bottom of the bath.

I carefully place the still frozen leg into a black bin bag, (pleased I thought of that) I place it on the floor before moving the shower curtain aside to allow me to arrange Jennifer's unconscious form with my plastic gloved hands (pleased I thought of those also) into a pose that implies an accidental fall.

Leaving the shower running I put the plug into the waste outlet, turning the taps on to allow the bath to fill quickly. Carefully supporting Jennifer's head until the water becomes of sufficient depth to allow her body to float, I raise her head further until I can push it back hard so her injured skull meets the edge of the roll top bath, leaving a clear mark of hair and blood on the rim. As I ease her head down the sloping side of the bath and back down into the water, I observe with some satisfaction the resulting evidence of the 'accident'.

I continue to hold her head under the rising water, air begins to escape from her nostrils and mouth, her eyes suddenly open and slowly focus on my own. At that moment a wave of guilt and sadness flows through my mind, this is the same girl I met on Brighton Pier, the daughter of George my surrogate father and the mother of my children. As these confused emotions and the moment of hesitation continue I realise that tears are flowing down my face and dripping into the bath water. As I continue to stare, my emotional confusion begins to disappear as I see that the look in her eyes is no longer the ugly, cruel glare that she had recently inherited from her mother, but was the kind and gentle look that I knew from our early life together. As her mouth twisted into a smile of affection I knew I was doing the right thing, I had saved her from her mother's evil influence, she would be welcomed by her loving father in a better place, I could sense his presence and encouragement. I smiled back lovingly at Jennifer as the life left her eyes and her face rested into a peaceful sleep.

Releasing her to float gently in the water, I turned off the bath taps, but left the shower to continue, stripped off the plastic gloves and my clothes and carefully put them into a separate bin bag. I then thoroughly wash and dress before carrying both bags downstairs to the kitchen.

My intention was to put both these bags into another single bag for disposal, but, as old frugal habits die hard I can't resist reaching in, cutting the plastic wrapper off the leg of lamb and placing it on a tray beside the sink to defrost ready for roasting later; as my mother always used to say, "waste not, want not!". Unfortunately, during this process, I had another pang of guilt as I realised the gross insult I had inflicted on Jennifer, the joint was not organic.

Dressed in my suit and coat I leave the house as usual with my brief case and the black bag that I planned to put into a skip near to the station. As I close the front door, the sound attracts the attention, as it does every morning, of our neighbour Mr Jeffries, who was sweeping his drive, which he does every morning at this time.

"Good morning" I shout, raising my hand in greeting, as I do every morning.

"Morning, is that you away off to work?" he replies, as he does every morning.

"No, I'm just going to find a skip to dispose of the evidence that I've just murdered Jennifer." Is the response that went through my head, but for the sake of routine I gave my normal reply.

"Yes, another day another dollar." We both chuckle, as we do every morning, before I continue my walk to the station, as I do every morning. Thank God, this monotonous routine is going to end soon.

CHAPTER 18

Diary note:

Monday evening. On the train going home. I was certain I could smell the Shepherd's Pie as I left the office, I think I'm developing a real phobia, an eating disorder would be the modern description, but I mustn't let these irritations rush my plans.

Good working day at the office, Valerie has booked a holiday in the South of France and is trying to learn how to speak the language.

Feel a little odd as part of me falsely believes that I have actually killed Jennifer. Trying to put this illogical thought aside and consider some of the issues and consequences of 'The Bathroom Accident' by continuing the process of 'what happens next'.

I visualised a scene in my office. Just before lunchtime, the phone buzzes and Valerie informs me, in a concerned voice, that there were two police officers in reception asking to see me. I told her to show them in.

Sergeant Dixon and Police Constable Green enter my office and introduce themselves, holding their caps in front of them nervously.

"Come in please and sit down," I greet them pleasantly, "how can I help you?" Valerie hovered in the doorway pretending she was waiting to see if we wanted some tea or coffee, but really just trying to glean a snippet of information that she could gossip about to her friends.

"Well sir, we'd prefer to stand," advised the sergeant, "I am sorry to advise you that your wife has had an accident."

"An accident?" I repeat with deep concern in my voice and expression on my face, "is she alright?"

"I'm afraid not," continued the sergeant with a sudden interest in his shoes as he struggled to hold eye contact, "your wife was found in your house having suffered an accident and has been pronounced dead by the doctors at Wexham Park Hospital. I am terribly sorry for your loss."

I sit back in my chair, tears welling up in my eyes.

"That's impossible, she was fine this morning when I left, she was getting ready to go shopping with her friend, I don't understand, what's happened? What sort of accident?" I stifle a sob over the word accident.

The Constable takes out his notebook after a nod from his sergeant.

"Mr Jeffries, a neighbour of yours, observed water exiting the house earlier today. Believing there was no one in the house and that a water pipe may have burst, he entered using a key that your wife had given him for use in an emergency. Mr Jeffries considered this to be such an occasion. He discovered your wife in the bathroom and called the emergency services. When we arrived with the ambulance, we found that your wife appeared to have slipped in the bath, I'm afraid there was very little we could do sir."

As I leave the train I continue my reverie, thinking through the whole episode to the end, even the part where I roasted the leg of lamb in the oven and served it to my grieving family who naturally assembled at our house; I even served a specially selected slice to Edith, who I was pleased to see was distraught, it was almost as if she could sense the impending misery I intended to inflict on her.

However, as I arrive home and Jennifer and I go through the usual routine of "Hello darling, I'm home. Something smells nice." "It's your favourite, Shepherd's Pie," some doubts have begun to creep into my mind as I recognise certain flaws and potential 'banana skins' that could occur in this 'household accident'. Firstly, what is the likelihood of the 'blunt instrument' connecting with the correct level of force and to the specific part of Jennifer's head that will firstly render her unconscious, and secondly, convince the police that the subsequent injury had been caused by her falling backwards against the edge of the bath. Finally, the injury to the front of her head where it inevitably collides with the wall when I hit her, this would certainly be a circumstance the police would find curious.

There are so many things that could go wrong. It is likely that the 'blunt instrument' doesn't connect as planned, if I miss and simply deliver a glancing blow, the whole 'accident' theme goes out the window as I would be forced to bludgeon her to death. It would then be obvious to even the most inept of investigating officer that the chances of her slipping and severely banging her head, not once but several times, in the bath is unlikely and they could inevitably only conclude that she'd been murdered.

Even if the single blow with the leg of lamb does have the desired effect and she does 'drop like a stone' as I visualised, will she remain passive and cooperative as I hold her head under the water to drown, she's more likely to start thrashing about, I simply don't have the experience and knowledge of what a victim does in these circumstances and I can't imagine there being a book or a website page on the subject. If I must use any force at all it's bound to leave marks on her, and again introduce doubts on the 'accidental' death conclusion that I'm trying to achieve.

Even if everything does go perfectly to plan, one of my most overriding doubts is whether I could hold Jennifer's head under the water and watch her die, it feels very cold blooded.

I smile to myself as I think of one of the true benefits of the whole scenario, I would at least get a good roast lamb dinner out of it, particularly if I did it on a Monday to avoid the dreaded Shepherd's Pie!

CHAPTER 19

Diary note:

Tuesday.

On the train going to work, bit of variety this morning as I left the house, Mr Jeffries's cat was run over by a passing cyclist, the cat appeared to be dead and the cyclist had hurt himself. Mr Jeffries was distraught, quite a crowd turned up to watch the drama and everyone seemed to enjoy themselves.

Feeling more positive today, I've decided to abandon all plans, for the time being, of creating a 'household accident' for Jennifer, having failed in my mind to kill her 'in the bath accident', or other visualisation of choking (on fish and chicken bones, cocktail sticks, even barbeque skewers), burning, electrocuting, shooting, stabbing, beating, drowning, crushing (with a wardrobe falling over onto her) and simply throwing her down the stairs. I believe I have exhausted all the potential options of 'The Household Accident'.

My next plan is to make her disappear, a simple plan; kill Jennifer, put her in the boot of the car, drive to a remote location, bury her and then report her missing. What could possibly go wrong,

---

I realised immediately as I tried to visualise each step of this plan, that precision and careful thought was needed to ensure its success and after several failed imaginary attempts to kill Jennifer, I believe I've worked out the details that will ensure a successful outcome. I close my eyes and allow this new plan to play out in my head.

One of the first things I must do, as I realise I have become quite office bound recently, is that my routine must change for this plan to succeed, so when I'm absent from the office it won't be quite so questionable. I'm therefore going to tell everyone in the office that I've taken up cycling and fishing, two sports that don't require any group involvement or club registration and will allow me to travel almost anywhere unquestioned.

It was now Wednesday night and I arrived home feeling quite excited, not for the routine drudgery of eating Jennifer's Macaroni and Cheese Bake, or the viewing of the same TV programmes that we sat watching brainlessly. No, tonight was the night, the planning and preparations were all complete, every detail had been considered, revised and reconsidered, the perfect murder was now about to be executed, I had no doubts, and felt very confident. The most important thing was to behave exactly as normal.

Last Sunday, when we had taken Edith home after the stringy, fatty and tasteless roast lamb Sunday lunch, I had removed from her bathroom cupboard one of the blister sleeves that contained 8 capsules from the box of her sleeping tablets. This had still left her with another blister sleeve containing 6 capsules, and as I knew she didn't take them often, I felt sure she wouldn't notice the shortfall or remember if she had used them herself or not. I was particularly careful in doing this, picking the box up and opening with a tissue and replacing it the same way, probably unnecessary but a precaution worth taking. The name on the box was Zopiclone 7.5mg and the instructions informed that 1 capsule an hour before bed would be sufficient to ensure a good night's sleep.

Later at home, I had emptied the fine white powder from each of the capsules into a small cellophane bag and carefully hidden it on top of a kitchen unit. The blister packaging and the capsule sleeves I put into another cellophane bag and disposed of it in a litter bin outside of Paddington Station on my way to work.

After Jennifer had served the Macaroni and Cheese and I had finally managed to clear my plate; Jennifer had eaten hers voraciously and had finished before I was even half way through mine. I stood to pour us another glass of wine, a rare treat for us on a weekday evening, but I served it with the explanation that I'd had a particularly successful day at the office and felt like celebrating, I could hardly tell her that the effects of the drugs would cause additional drowsiness when taken with alcohol, as I'd discovered on-line. Before sitting down, I told her to sit and enjoy her wine and I would serve her the rice pudding for a change.

"Thank you Philip, I'm feeling really spoilt," was her reply as she raised her glass.

I went to the kitchen, lifted the rice pudding from the oven, spooned a small portion into Jennifer's bowl, retrieved the small cellophane bag and sprinkled the contents over the sweet, milky desert. I then spooned more into the bowl, carefully mixing it all together. I filled my own bowl before returning to the table, constantly repeating in my head 'Jennifer in left hand, Jennifer in left hand!' The bowl had hardly been placed in front of her before her spoon was moving with the speed of woodpecker.

"This is delicious, as usual," I declared, "would you like some more?" noticing that her bowl was being scrapped.

"I think I will," as she headed towards the kitchen, knowing there was no point in me following her as I knew she would finish it all off, such a pity as it was one of the highlight dishes of the week.

Within half an hour I could see Jennifer beginning to doze in her chair in front of the TV, it was 'Autumn Watch', which is enough to send anyone off to sleep, but tonight I suspected it was the 8 sleeping tablets that were to blame.

I waited another hour, Jennifer had become very still, her head slouched forward, and I could see that her face had become so relaxed that drool was oozing out of the corner of her mouth and running down the crease at the side of her chin. I knelt beside her, listening carefully, her breathing was very slow and light, not the rasping snoring that I was used to hearing whilst she slumbered. I shook her by the shoulders, gently at first and then quite rigorously, but her breathing never changed and she showed no sign of being disturbed.

I went back through the kitchen and utility room and into the garage, closing all the window blinds and propping open the doors as I passed. Taking one of two large sheets of grey, heavy duty polythene that I had bought from the garden centre, I opened the boot of the car and carefully spread it out, so it covered all surfaces. I then took the second piece of polythene, three towels and a roll of duct tape from the shelf and returned to the sitting room, pausing at the door to observe my unconscious wife. I smiled when I saw that the TV was now showing an episode of CSI!

I unrolled the polythene sheet on the floor in front of Jennifer's chair, spread out two of the towels, one on top of each other, half way down, and stood to begin the task of moving Jennifer out of the chair and laying her onto the towels and polythene. This proved considerably easier than I had imagined, she was so floppy that as soon as I pulled her forward by the shoulders, she just slid, with some guidance and support, onto the floor, never making a sound, apart from a light grunt and a small fart. She was so comatose I had to again check to see if she'd already died, but she hadn't.

I rolled her over, so she was face down, and squatted over her upper torso, lent forward and with one hand I held her nose and with the other sealed her mouth. I held on tightly and waited, her body made two small twitches, which made me apply greater pressure. Not knowing how long this would take, I just held on and waited, but when I noticed that CSI had come to an end, I felt certain that Jennifer would've probably come to an end as well.

I released my grip and moved to a kneeling position beside her, I checked her breathing – nothing. I checked her pulse – nothing. I had definitely killed her, and it had taken so little effort and stress, I could hardly believe it, there hadn't even been a need for the towels as she hadn't soiled herself, as I felt sure she would. I carefully and meticulously wrapped her up in the polythene, thoroughly binding and sealing the edges with the duct tape. Laying out the third towel, a large one that I remember we had taken to the beach one summers day with a picnic, that had been a wonderful day, it had been warm and sunny, Jennifer had gone 'topless' and we'd shared egg sandwiches and a pork pie, then '99's' from the ice cream van.

Rolling Jennifer's tightly bound corpse over onto the towel and holding the edges, I pulled, easily sliding it across the wood and lino floors, across the sitting room, through the kitchen and utility room, gliding to a halt at the garage door. It was here I expected greater difficulty, lifting her from the floor and into the boot of the car and my expectations were certainly realised. I understood what they meant by 'a dead weight', and after 10 minutes of lifting, pulling and pushing, perspiration running down my face, I finally succeeded.

A couple of nights ago I had woken myself up, I had, in my dream, been rehearsing the murder and everything had been going well. The dream, however, turned into a nightmare when it came to getting Jennifer back out of the car because I'd simply laid her out as flat as possible. When it came to lift her out, all the floppiness had disappeared, and she was rigid with rigor mortice, her feet were trapped under one side of the boot and her head and shoulders wedged under the other. No matter what I tried or how much effort I expended, she remained stuck.

Eventually I had to amputate her legs from the knees downwards, what a bloody mess and all my efforts to leave no evidence was ruined.

So, with the benefit of this nocturnal knowledge, I positioned Jennifer in more of a foetal position. This had two advantages, the first being I would be able to get her out, the second was that she would sit better in the wheel barrow, that I would need later. Having closed the boot, opened the garage door and drove out the car and parked it in the drive, as I had done every Thursday for the past few weeks.

Now, as I usually would, I locked the house up, turned off the TV and the lights, ironed a shirt, set out my clothes for tomorrow, brushed my teeth and went to bed, almost immediately falling asleep.

The next morning, I continued my normal routine; most important not to do anything different. I then walked to the station, exactly as I always did, at exactly the usual time, speaking to Mr Jeffries, as usual, who was sweeping his drive, as usual, apart from when he's dealing with a dead cat.

CHAPTER 20

Diary note:

Thursday morning, on the train going to work. I feel a momentous release, almost joyous, I don't know why I've left it for 27 years to make these positive plans to improve my life. My thoughts and dreams have been so real I again almost believe that I have killed Jennifer. I am going to do a 10-minute meditation to bring me back to reality, people have been looking at me suspiciously, they're obviously not used to seeing me grinning inanely.

Going to continue with planning and reviewing, in my mind, the next stages of Jennifer's 'disappearance'. So far all seems to be going well.

For many weeks, I had been exploring on my bike, on foot, in the car and while fishing, trying to source a location to dispose of Jennifer. It was while visiting a major new commercial client just off the M4 at Theale that the ideal solution presented itself. His premises were some distance from the nearest railway station, certainly far enough to justify using the car. It was on my first visit that I found the perfect spot, having had some fishing recommended by the client and gone exploring after the meeting. I followed the road towards Pangbourne and when I observed signs for trout fishing, I turned off and followed a little road that eventually, after many twists and turns, arrived at a very pretty and peaceful location; a fisherman's hut and a series of small lakes with manicured landscaping around. The place was completely deserted, Thursday in November was obviously not the most popular of fishing times. It was certainly a place I intended to return and enjoy some sport.

I sat in the car for a while, enjoying the view and the tranquillity of the environment, before leaving and retracing my route, this time paying much greater attention to the surroundings and soon found the elusive 'perfect spot'. Behind the trees, almost completely hidden, was a small car park, obviously for weekend walkers. I drove in and parked, getting out of the car and walking around the perimeter, observing the several well-worn footpaths that led away into the woodland and immediately realised the potential of this isolated location. I decided that I would return every Thursday, on the pretext of visiting the client or going fishing, to prepare Jennifer's final resting place.

I made notes of exactly what I had done this day for future reference; driving the car out of the garage the night before, usual train to work, leaving work at 1.00pm and taking the train back to Slough, walking into the drive, briefcase on the back seat, not entering the house but driving off for either the regular appointment at Theale or fishing on the Pangbourne lakes.

On the next Thursday, I realised that my neighbour, Mr Jeffries seemed to be on permanent 'patrol' at this time, busy doing jobs in the garden. He was most curious as to what I was doing home.

"Hello Phillip, you've missed Jennifer, she left 20 minutes ago."

"Hello Mr Jeffries, no problem, I didn't expect her to be home, she was going shopping this afternoon. I've just come to pick up the car before I go to visit a client in Theale. I'm then going for a fly fishing lesson, I'm taking up trout fishing." I replied.

"Fishing, I never thought of you as a fisherman, but I'm always happy to share your catch." He chuckled.

"I think it'll be a little while before I'm likely to catch anything, but if I do, you'll be the first to know!" I drove off, leaving the nosey old bastard to his everlasting chores. I realised however, that his regular presence as a future witness could be very important.

After my second meeting at Theale, I stopped at a DIY store and bought sheets of polythene, duct tape, a pick, a shovel, a wheelbarrow, a roll of black bin bags, blue overalls, a pair of work boots, a box of disposable plastic gloves and a box of disposable plastic shoe covers. I then drove to my secret location, parked the car, removed my suit jacket and trousers, shirt, tie, shoes and socks in the car. Swinging my legs out of the door and standing on one of the polythene bags, I put on my 'working gear'. I thought by always going through this routine I would avoid the possibility of any evidence associated with this location contaminating the car or my clothes.

Taking the tools, wheelbarrow and half a dozen bin bags, I set of for 'the chosen place', which was about 150m into the wood, not near any paths and where the shrubbery and undergrowth became quite dense and would conceal perfectly the excavation I intended to undertake. I first scraped around and filled several of the bags with the detritus lying on the surface; leaves, twigs, etc and placed them securely under a bush.

The smell of the newly excavated soil reminded me of when I helped my step father in his allotment, I loved those days, just him and me, turning the soil over and working it into a fine tilth before preparing and planting seedlings of vegetables and flowers that we nurtured and harvested for the house. Until that day when we sat on the bench seat in his allotment drinking a cup of tea from his flask. He had been particularly troubled and unusually quiet that day, and we sat in silence for some time, before he asked in a voice that was full of emotion, "Do you know where Alice has gone?" I didn't really want to answer this question because I knew exactly where she was.

I willed myself to stop thinking about this awkward time in my life, deciding I must stop distracting myself with thoughts from the past and focus on the task at hand, that of preparing Jennifer's final resting place.

Having bagged up the surface leaves at 'the grave site' I commenced digging, not as easy as I thought it would be, the roots and shale soil proved quite resistant and after an hour, my programmed time limit, I had only created a shallow trench some 2m long x half a metre wide and deep. The soil, piled up on one side had already created a sizeable mound and I wondered if later I may have to barrow some away as the excavation reached its intended 1.8 metre depth. I placed the tools and the upended barrow in the trench and retraced my steps back to the car. Putting on a pair of disposable gloves I opened the car door, then removed all my work gear while standing on an open plastic bag, and sitting back in the car, removing the disposable gloves before touching anything, and putting them in the bag with the work clothes, I swung my feet in and redressed with my 'office clothes'. Putting on a fresh pair of disposable gloves and a pair of shoe protectors, I stepped out of the car, opened a new bin bag, inserted the other that contained all my working clothes, removed the plastic gloves and inserted the sealed bag in the boot and set off home.

On the drive back, I allowed my mind to drift back to that time sitting on the bench in the allotment with my Foster Father, Jack; what a nice man, he always did his best, but never had a clue what was going on under his roof and hated any form of conflict or disagreement. Alice, who was a year older than me, was also being fostered by Jack and our foster mother, Sheila. Sheila was the greatest cook; soups and cakes being her speciality, she was kind, caring and gentle. Both our foster parents wanted us to be happy and allowed us a great deal of freedom, which both Alice and I took advantage of.

Alice was wilful, deceitful, beautiful and even though she was only fourteen, her body was very well developed, and she was always quite happy to show me her 'bits'. It took some persuasion to get me to show her my 'bits', as I knew it was wrong, and I still worried that by committing even the smallest "pleasure of the skin", my journey to the fiery pits of hell would be assured. However, once we were both 'exposed' the journey down the slippery slopes of her breasts to the fun palace in the south, was a magical experience that we were soon engaging in at every opportunity. Did we ever discuss birth control – No. What did that mean?

When Alice became quiet, subdued and refused suddenly to even talk to me, I thought I had upset her in some way. Finally, I forced her to tell me what was wrong, and she screamed back at me.

"I'm pregnant, I'm going to have a baby and it's all your fault, I thought because we're young it couldn't happen to us and since you're such a little boy, I thought it was impossible, so it's all your fault." I couldn't understand how exactly it was entirely my fault, but I felt her anger, hurt, fear and shame, and as I loved her with all my heart, I embraced and accepted all the blame. Alice stood crying into her hands, I looked down at my feet without any idea of what to say. Alice soon recovered from her crying and began to shout at me again.

"You're such a little boy, you just stand there and do nothing, say nothing, I hate you and it's all your fault." I tried and tried to think of something to say, and then, of course, it was obvious, what had taken me so long to think of it.

"Will you marry me?" I asked with a loving smile, which was soon wiped from my face as Alice's hand connected with my cheek with ferocious speed, knocking me sideways, allowing her to stride past me, with a final insult.

"Stupid little boy."

I heard nothing about anything from anybody, but for ages there was a sombre atmosphere throughout the house, meals were eaten in silence, conversations held in whispers, I guessed from this that Jack and Sheila knew of Alice's secret.

Two weeks went by in this tense household environment before, very late one-night, Alice woke me up, crawled under my blankets and whispered.

"I only told Sheila that I was having a baby, I wouldn't tell her who the father was so you're not in trouble, they don't know it's you. Tomorrow I'm going to see a doctor who's going to take it away." Alice's hand had slid from my chest, down over my stomach and began playing with the very equipment that had got her into so much trouble already. "I can't get pregnant again now, so we're absolutely safe and I want to do it with you one last time." So, we did, and we never did again. But I carried the feeling of shame of what I had done and guilt that I hadn't either admitted to Sheila or Jack my role in this crisis or supported Alice in some way. It was the day that Alice went to see the doctor that Jack and I sat in the allotment, drinking tea and smelling the newly turned earth, in silence, before he asked me that question.

"Do you know where Alice has gone?" I wanted to answer this question truthfully and take responsibility for my sin. I wanted Jack to put his arm around me and tell me that we all make mistakes. I wanted his reassurance that everything was going to be alright and our lives would return to normal, but I was certain that if I admitted I knew where Alice had gone, all of our lives would change and would never be the same again. I also believed that as Alice hadn't told anyone that I was to blame, it would be a betrayal of her wishes. My answer was simple.

"No?" I replied, as if it was a question. Jack paused before putting his arm around me and to end any further discussion he nodded his head and said.

"That's good, I'm so pleased." He then got up signalling that it was time for us to continue our work in the garden.

It took me six Thursdays to complete the grave, plus two other Thursdays when I did actually have fishing lessons and tried to catch a fish, without any success. I always approached the area with caution knowing that if someone had discovered my work, they would have left evidence and probably removed the tools, but every time things were undisturbed and as I left them.

So, as I returned home from the office on the final Thursday lunchtime, I met Mr Jeffries, as usual. Today he was cutting the hedge, I did offer to cut our side this weekend, but he kindly offered to continue and cut the whole hedge if I didn't mind, how could I refuse. I waved to him as I drove off in the car with my 'cargo' in the boot.

The meeting with the client was quite short, but very successful, all the contracts had been signed and it was really a simple matter of hand shaking and smiles. After I left, I immediately went to 'the chosen place'.

After going through my careful undressing and dressing routine, I firstly went to the 'grave site', checked all was undisturbed and returned to the car with the wheelbarrow, opened the boot and with a great deal of struggling managed to load a very rigid and unyielding Jennifer into the wheel barrow. Looking about very anxiously, this was not a good moment to be disturbed by anyone, I pushed her, balanced very precariously on the wheelbarrow, the 150 metres into the woods, quickly and with little further difficulty. Without any ceremony, I tipped her into the hole, landing with a sludgy splash at the bottom. A perfect fit. I lowered the wheelbarrow into the hole as well as the pick before shovelling the soil back, regularly stamping to compact it. After a final levelling and tidying up, I emptied and spread the bags of leaves and woodland debris I had stored in bags over the entire area before retreating back to the car. I again went through the undressing, dressing procedure, as well as wrapping the shovel in a plastic bag and putting it in the boot with my bagged clothing and work shoes before folding the protective plastic sheet around everything, tying and sealing it with duct tape.

I left without a backwards glance and drove home, only stopping once to put my 'package' into a skip on the outskirts of Slough.

As I drove into my drive, stopping the car in front of the garage, it was almost dark. Mr Jeffries was finishing off raking and sweeping up after the hedge cutting and I walked over to him.

"Mr Jeffries, that was very kind of you, you've made a wonderful job and it's most appreciated."

"No problem," he replied, "I know how busy you and Jennifer are, so I thought it was the least I could do."

"Well thank you again, would you like a cup of tea or, as it's getting late, how about a beer?" I asked. He looked at his watch.

"Ah! What the hell, it's not tea time yet, a beer is a great idea, I'll just finish up and come straight over."

I went into the house, turned on some lights, opened the garage door, drove the car in and parked. I then went to the kitchen and opened two bottles of beer, pouring them into glasses just as Mr Jeffries knocked at the front door and let himself in.

"Come into the kitchen," I shouted," I've got a couple of beers ready." As Mr Jeffries came in and sat at the table I explained that I wasn't sure where Jennifer was, but I'm sure she'd be back soon.

As we sat talking Mr Jeffries told me of his various health problems and the indefinite wait he was experiencing for treatment on the NHS and how he struggled to support his wife; her dementia, which had rapidly got worse over the past 12 months had meant that she could no longer be left alone for very long. For someone who couldn't leave his wife alone for too long, and as he began to finish a second beer, I began to wonder who was looking after her. As if by telepathy the same thought obviously crossed his mind and he stood up, I thanked him again and he left.

I waited until seven thirty before I started making phone calls. I called Edith first, who replied angrily to my enquiry as to whether Jennifer was with her.

"Don't be stupid, she never comes around on a Thursday," and put the phone down to prevent any further discussion. I then called the charity shop where Jennifer helped out a couple of times a week, but the answer machine spoke to me advising of the opening times and how to donate. I left a brief message asking if Jennifer was there working late, and if she was, could she give me a call. I then called my daughter Susanne, we spoke for some while and she was very concerned as she knew how rigid her mother was in her routines. I thought that 'rigid' was an extremely good description under the circumstances. I promised to call her back when she came in and that I would call David; a similar conversation followed with him. All he could say was that he couldn't think where she could be, "she's always at home and she's bound to come back soon."

I called the vicarage, The Meals on Wheels helpline and everyone else I could think of. At 8.30 I called the local police station and explained the situation, that Jennifer was always home by six o'clock at the latest and it was now very late, I had already rung everywhere I thought she could be, but she seemed to be missing.

I could hear the policeman's thoughts;

'She's probably in the sack with her toy boy.'

'She'll have run away with her yoga teacher.'

But he actually told me that it was too soon for the police to become involved, there would certainly be a simple explanation for her lateness and he was sure she would be home soon. I insisted this wasn't right, she wasn't the type of person not to be at home at this time of night. I asked for his name and to speak with a senior officer. He readily gave me his name and number but advised that he was the duty sergeant and there were no more senior officers available. I thanked him and apologised for being irate, but it had been out of genuine concern and worry. He again reassured me that he was certain the situation would resolve itself and if she was still missing tomorrow, to call again and the police could become involved. I thanked him again and asked him to make a note of Jennifer's and my own details in case he heard anything.

I called Susanne and David again to tell them of my conversation with the police, none of us could think of anything further that could be done but wait. Susanne decided that she should come over and wait with me and no matter what I said, she couldn't be dissuaded. 'Shit', I thought, I was going to drink another couple of beers, order a takeaway and have a quiet night watching some television, none of which was appropriate with Susanne coming here, fretting and fussing.

CHAPTER 21

Diarynote:

Friday. On my way to work. Feeling positive.

What a great plan, it's simple and completely under my control. I think is fool proof, but I'm going to give thoughts as to what is likely to happen next.

After sitting up most of the night, a most uncomfortable experience, with Susanne, who had duly turned up at 9.30 on that Thursday evening. We discussed, albeit briefly as there wasn't many options, what could've happened to her mother, every theory she put forward seemed implausible and having run out of any ideas, we waited, unfortunately not in silence. I was expected to listen to a constant barrage of incessant words exiting Susanne's mouth, inane, boring stuff about the children and their school, her friends, her house, her car, on and on she went, I can hardly remember anything she said, all I can remember was that tired feeling that comes through lack of interest and lack of sleep, almost like you have a cold coming on. Her head finally rested back in the chair and she fell asleep. For about five minutes there was peace and I began to relax and allow my mind to settle, five minutes of peace before she started snoring, a harsh rattling snore that would have made a drunken Irish navvy proud.

"For fucks sake," I thought, "Is there no end to my misery?" As I sat looking at her I realised how different she was to her mother when she was 26, Susanne had more the features and mannerisms of a middle-aged Jennifer, but without any charisma. Certainly, Susanne's snoring had an edge on her mother's abilities. I must have dozed off myself as I was suddenly awoken by Susanne shaking my shoulder.

"Dad, wake up, you're snoring so loudly you'll wake the neighbours!" I felted slighted by this apparent injustice, but apologised and sat back up in the chair; God forbid that I should disturb Susanne's rumblings.

So, we sat and waited, and waited, until after what seemed like an eternity, morning arrived, and Susanne awoke again after having fallen asleep in the early hours. As Jennifer had, surprisingly, not returned home, Susanne asked in a croaky voice,

"What are we going to do?"

"I don't know darling, I've been thinking all night where she could be." I put my face in my hands dramatically and finished with an emotional whisper, "I just don't know where she can be or what to do, I've been praying she's alright." Susanne, in a surprisingly sympathetic gesture, moved over and put her arms around me and suggested we go down to the police station together.

The police still advised us that it was still less than 24 hours, which is the time they believed should be allowed before they would normally become involved, unless it was a minor or someone that may be at risk, and as Jennifer fitted in neither of the categories there was nothing they could do at present. Susanne became quite aggressive and insisted that as it had now been more than 24 hours since anyone saw her, the police should involve themselves immediately; she then stood glaring at the poor sergeant, who had no choice but accept her argument. We were shown to an interview room by a young constable who filled out a form, rather disinterestedly, asking simple questions like name, address, age, when we saw her last etc. We were then advised to go home and wait; a CID officer would be in touch to arrange another interview, so they could begin their enquiries.

We returned home, I called Edith and David to tell them what was happening, Edith, ever the thoughtless, selfish bitch, asked sternly.

"Jennifer always comes around and gives me my lunch on a Friday, so she'd better be found quickly, or you'll have to arrange for someone else to bring me my lunch."

I got a much more sympathetic and understanding response when I rang the office and explained the situation to Valerie, who agreed to cancel all my appointments and insisted I call if I needed anything; there were somethings that crossed my mind but nothing appropriate.

Susanne and I then sat and waited. We drank cups of coffee, then some tea and then some more coffee and we waited. We both agreed we weren't hungry, so we had no lunch. I was absolutely bloody starving but felt that to admit this would show a lack of compassion.

At four o'clock the phone rang, it was a voice that would come to haunt me over the coming months, a voice that introduced itself as Detective Inspector Richards who stated, not asked, that he would come around to the house in about an hour to complete the paperwork with regards to my wife's disappearance.

Susanne stayed, she wanted to be part of this evolving drama, I did suggest that although we weren't hungry and didn't feel like eating, we ought to have something as it could be another long evening and night. Susanne agreed, but did she get her fat arse out of the chair to prepare anything for her distraught father? no chance! I finally raised myself and went through to the kitchen, where I began making scrambled eggs on toast for the two of us, in the space of time it took me to prepare this I also prepared and ate two ham sandwiches and a packet of crisps. I called Susanne and we sat quietly eating. When we finished she announced.

"I'm going to call Ian and update him on what's happening," and she left to use the phone. This reminded me of all the years this lazy little bitch had lived at home, after every meal she would announce she had to do her homework, or she had to get her gym stuff ready, or she had to do this or that; always something to get out of doing the dishes or any form of household chore. I wondered how things worked with Ian and her own misbehaving brats at home. I washed the dishes and put them away, eating two chocolate biscuits as compensation.

At five fifteen, DI Richards arrived, a dour faced man, in his early fifties with a demeanour that announced, 'I've seen it all before and I don't believe you'. We sat at the kitchen table and without any pleasantries he immediately demanded a recent photograph of Jennifer, which I had anticipated and passed one over to him. His slightly bulbous eyes moved over the photo before returning to stare at me, a stare that seemed to travel between my chin, mouth, cheeks and eyes making me feel uncomfortable, it was as if he knew everything and could see my guilt. His pale face hinted towards a bluish hue and showed a lifestyle of long hours, poor diet and a close friendship with Johnnie Walker and his many friends. His demeanour displayed a patience that came from hours of listening to lies. A patience that was always rewarded when the truth was uncovered.

With his notebook resting on his knee with practised balance, he began by explaining that much of the information he needed, and therefore many of the questions he would be asking, may appear to be either irrelevant or even offensive at this stressful time, but he had to ask them, as a matter of routine, to hopefully rule out several possibilities to explain why Mrs Chamber's was missing. Again, his eyes scanned between Susanne and myself; he asked without any further introduction.

"Why do you think your wife's gone missing?" My mouth opened to reply but Susanne spoke up first.

"We cannot think of any reason, she has a very organised life and she always does everything at the same time every day."

"That's absolutely right," I continued, "she does her charity work, she helps at the church and does the garden and her household chores, she hardly ever goes out in the evening by herself and is always here when I come home from work, so I cannot think of where she is."

"When was the last time you saw her?"

"I saw her on Wednesday afternoon, about four o'clock," replied Susanne, "she stopped by to have a cup of tea, I remember because the children had just got home from school."

"And you Mr Chambers, when was the last time you saw your wife?" his tone was accusatory. "I didn't have to lie, the last time I saw Jennifer was just before I wrapped her up in the polythene sheeting.

"It was Wednesday evening when we went to bed." The DI immediately seized on the fact that I hadn't seen her on the Thursday morning.

"You went to bed on the Wednesday night and didn't see her again, why was that?"

"Jennifer and I have separate bedrooms and I never disturb her in the mornings as I go off to work early."

"Separate bedrooms," the DI stated with a questioning eyebrow raised, "did you have some marital problems?"

"No, nothing like that, it just suited us better, we didn't disturb each other." The DI didn't seem convinced and just looked at me before making a note in his book.

"How would you describe your relationship with your wife?"

"Very good, we both went about our daily lives and are both content, we got on very well, we've been together for a long time." I replied taking care to use the word 'are' instead of, as I nearly did, 'were'. The DI again made a note before asking Susanne.

153

"And did you have a good relationship with your mother?"

"Very good," she replied, "Mum has always been very supportive and generous, particularly with the children."

"When you say supportive, was she lending or giving you money?" Susanne immediately became flustered and her face flushed.

"No, well, Yes," she replied, "Mum had given us some money lately because our car had broken, and we needed to buy a new one. I didn't mean it like that, I meant she always listened to my problems and was supportive in everything I did."

"Do you have financial problems at home, did you need more money from your mother?"

"Detective Inspector," I immediately interrupted, "I don't want you to waste time with this line of enquiry, whenever any of the family needed help, either financial or otherwise, Jennifer and I always discussed it and agreed to give whatever support we could. Can we focus on finding Jennifer?" Susanne looked at me gratefully.

"That is what I'm trying to do," replied the DI gruffly, "and it's very important that I fully understand Mrs Chamber's relationships to get a picture of what may have caused her to go missing." He continued to question Susanne.

"After you'd had your tea with your mother on Wednesday afternoon, was there anything that seemed different about her, was she troubled or worried about anything?"

"No, she was just normal, she mentioned she was going shopping the following morning, she asked if there was anything I needed."

"And was there?" asked the DI. My god, I thought, this guy doesn't give up.

"No, there was nothing, I don't think she was going for anything specific herself, she just always went shopping on a Thursday." The DI made some more notes before his attention turned back to me.

"Did you know your wife went shopping every Thursday, whether she needed anything or not?" I paused, I couldn't quite think of how best to answer his question.

"I'm sure when she went shopping she went for a reason, I think it was usually groceries, sometimes clothes and sometimes she stopped by at the charity shop she helped out in and had a coffee."

"Are you certain that's what she did on a Thursday?" again he raised his questioning eyebrow.

"It's what she always told me, and I had no reason to believe she did anything else." I replied a little defensively.

"Could she have been meeting with a 'special' friend every Thursday, Mr Chambers? Had she been conducting a relationship with someone else, another man, perhaps?"

"Not a chance, that's out of the question, how dare you even suggest such a thing," I replied indignantly, the thought of anyone wanting to have an affair with Jennifer was ridiculous, but I quite liked the idea that the DI may consider it a possibility.

"You say, 'not a chance', was your wife not an attractive woman, could she not have been secretly having an affair, do you really know what your wife is doing while you're at work?" Again, I didn't know how best to answer his questions, they were so manipulative.

"I'm just certain that I'd know," I blustered. The DI made some more notes in his book, I glanced across at Susanne, she seemed shocked and confused at how the interview was going.

"You said the last time you saw your wife was on Wednesday evening when you went to bed, was there anything odd or different about her behaviour, did she seem distracted or preoccupied in anyway?"

"Not really, she'd had some cross words with the Vicar and the church committee about changes to the flower arranging rota and that seemed to be distracting her, but nothing else in particular, we ate our supper, watched some television and went to bed; just our normal routine."

"What did you have for your supper?" he asked.

"Jennifer had cooked macaroni and cheese, we always had that on Wednesday."

"What did you watch on the TV?"

"We watched Autumn Watch and then CSI, but I was reading some papers at the same time, but those are two that I remember." I was beginning to feel this interview turning into an interrogation, but reminded myself to remain calm, patient and focussed. The DI sat making notes, I didn't quite know what he was writing down, but there was a pause of five minutes before his pen finally stopped moving and he again looked up.

"And that's all you did last night, nothing else?"

"No, that was it. Oh, I remember I put the car in the drive because I was going to an afternoon meeting in Theale and needed the car."

"Why did you do that?" the DI was instantly suspicious, "why didn't you get the car out in the morning or before you left in the afternoon?"

"Jennifer always complained that if I got the car out in the morning early it woke her up. When I returned to collect the car in the afternoon, she also thought it would much more convenient and save me having to go through the house twice; unlocking the doors, getting the car out, then relocking it all again for the sake of getting the car out the evening before."

"I can't work out the logic of that, it seems an odd thing to do." He paused, thinking of his next question. "How often did you have to do this car manoeuvre; did you regularly go to meetings in your car?"

"I've had regular Thursday meetings with a new client in Theale, I think for the past seven or eight weeks, I prefer to take the train wherever I can, so I don't use the car often, but this client is too far from the railway station, it's much more convenient to drive." Again, the DI paused and made more notes before continuing.

"So, you got up on the Thursday morning, what time was that and what did you do until your afternoon meeting?"

"I got up at 6.45, showered, shaved, got dressed, went downstairs, put my coat on and left for the railway station."

"You didn't have any breakfast? Not even a cup of tea?"

"No, I always buy a coffee at the station and drink it on the train. There's always croissants and pastries at the office if I want something to eat."

"Did you see or speak to anyone on the way to the station."

"No." I simply replied; a stupid question in my book, who the hell speaks to each other at seven o'clock in the morning on the way to work, certainly not this arsehole policeman, I'd be surprised if anyone spoke to him at any time of the day!

"Oh!" I pretended to remember, "I did briefly say good morning to Mr Jeffries next door, he's always about early. I then took the train and got to work just after eight. We were busy all morning and I left about twelve thirty, took the train home, got in the car and drove to my meeting at Theale."

"Did you see Jennifer when you went home to collect the car, or did you see or speak to anyone between leaving the office and arriving in Theale?"

"I bought a sandwich from 'Pret a Manger' at the station, and yes, when I got home Mr Jeffries was cutting the hedge and offered to cut our side as well and we had a brief conversation before I drove off." The DI made more notes as I waited for his next question.

"What time was your meeting at Theale?"

"Two thirty and it lasted about 40 minutes."

"It seems a lot of effort and long way to go, what was the purpose of your meeting?"

"I went to complete the signing of documents, they're a new and very valuable client and it's a large commercial policy for his diverse business requirements," I replied, believing this response was sufficiently mundane to be of no interest to him, how wrong could I be!

"When you say policy, is that an insurance policy, are you an insurance broker?"

160

"Insurance broker would be an oversimplification, we offer specialised and bespoke policies and financial instruments, but yes, we sell insurance."

"Did you have insurance on the life of your wife?"

"Yes, of course, we both have life policies."

"Are they large policies and have you changed or increased them recently?" It was obvious from the look of the DI's face that he definitely thought he had found the motive for Jennifer's disappearance.

"Yes, they are quite large policies and we've had them for a number of years and are reviewed annually. I'm happy for you to look at the policies and you can see for yourself the value and details. I must say, you are making me feel very uncomfortable, as if I'm responsible in some way for Jennifer being missing." I stated indignantly. The DI ignored my protest and just continued.

"Who would benefit from these policies if anything were to happen to you or your wife?" I breathed out heavily to show my irritation before remembering my promise to remain calm.

"That is detailed in each of our wills, principally the surviving spouse would inherit, but effectively the whole family would benefit from the inheritance." He paused again to make notes before continuing with his questions.

"What time did you arrive home?"

"It was just before six o'clock."

"Really?" exclaimed the DCI, "your meeting started at two-thirty and lasted forty minutes you said," glancing at his notebook for confirmation. "That makes the time about three- fifteen, it would take about forty minutes to drive home, so you should've been back by four o'clock. What did you do during those other two hours?"

"I went fishing for a little while at some lakes near Pangbourne, which are not far from my client's offices. I took up fishing there on the his recommendation and I take every opportunity to enjoy the sport, it's very peaceful and relaxing."

"Did you see or meet anyone there."

"No, not that I remember."

"So, you arrived home at about six, what happened then and at what point did you begin to have concerns about your wife?" I explained about my conversation with Mr Jeffries and him drinking a beer, which I had offered as a way of thanking him for the work he'd done on the hedge. How I really began to get concerned after seven o'clock, Jennifer was never that late, so I called different people, including the police station, David my son and of course Susanne." I looked over at her and smiled. "She came over straightaway and we have been waiting here ever since." We again sat in silence while the DI continued to write his notes before he finally closed his book and explained.

"I need you to give me all the contact details for your wife's charity works, including the church, as well as all her family members and friends. If you can let me have that by tomorrow morning, I will complete the necessary paperwork and begin an enquiry to locate Mrs Chambers. Obviously, in the meantime, if she returns or you discover yourself where she is, you must let us know immediately. I will contact you again shortly to arrange for you to attend the station and complete a formal statement.", the DI stood ready to leave as he was telling us this, but I delayed him.

"I have prepared a list of all the contact details of family, friends, charity contacts and other people that she's acquainted with," I passed him a hand written A4 sheet with the information, "and if you wait a few minutes I'll give you our life policies, so you have everything." I went through to my desk in the sitting room and returned, handing him the policies."

"You seem to be unusually and exceptionally well prepared, Mr Chambers," he stated with a suspicious tone. With a final, "I'll be in touch," he turned and left.

Susanne and I breathed a sigh of relief. We discussed how DI Richards had made us both feel guilty and responsible in some way, and how we both felt completely exhausted. It was now getting quite late and Susanne decided to go home to put the children to bed and as she drove off, I waved to her from the front-door.

CHAPTER 22

I had looked forward to this moment for so long, I leant my back against the door and this time breathed a genuine sigh of relief. I had the house completely to myself, the hallway seemed to echo as I walked through it, pausing before picking up the phone; I smiled, no fucking fish that had been steamed for twenty four hours served with watery, tasteless vegetables smeared with a lumpy cheese sauce, Jennifer's usual offering on a Friday night, for me tonight. No, it was going to by an Indian feast; my favourite selection of a Chicken Tikka starter with crispy lettuce and a mint dressing, followed by Lamb Jalfrezi with Pilau Rice, a Sag Aloo and a Peshwari Nan. Just to quench my thirst, I ordered four icy cold Cobra beers. It felt great to realise I could eat the whole meal without interruption or demands from Jennifer to share, I never understood why she always ordered something I didn't like, but then always wanted "just a taste", which meant half, of mine.

I had worked up quite an appetite, between all the waiting throughout the day, Susanne's questions and constant chatter, the phone calls to, and return calls from, work colleagues, friends, relatives, all expressing their support and concerns for the anxiety I must be suffering. The most exhausting, of course, had been the interview with DI Richards, but now, having poured the largest gin and tonic my glass would take, I relaxed and congratulated myself, I believed all had gone very well, a perfect end to a perfect plot. With the football match on the TV, I sat in pleasurable contentment, relishing the taste of the delicious hot and spicy food, quenching its heat with cool mouthfuls of icy beer.

I slept very soundly that night.

CHAPTER 23

Unfortunately, my personal pleasure lasted for less than twenty-four hours.

I'd awoken a little later than normal, a new start meant a change in routine, did it not? I showered but didn't shave as I felt the neglected look would benefit my image. I was downstairs by eight thirty and just pottered happily about the house, humming cheery little tunes, until the phone calls began. Susanne first – no news, David was next – no news, the third phone call caught me a bit by surprise, it was DI Richards. He explained, in a raspy, smokers voice, that he had some more questions to ask and would come around in about thirty minutes. What could I say? I know what I felt like saying!

As good as his word the DI arrived thirty minutes later but surprised me by being accompanied by a DS Edwards and two uniformed officers, one with an Alsatian dog, that looked as friendly as DI Richards.

"Can we come in?" the DI asked authoritatively as if he intended to, whatever my reply. Once inside, again in the same official tone, he asked if they could look around the house, he hoped they may find some clues that would explain Jennifer's disappearance. Although I knew there was nothing for them to discover, I didn't want to just roll over and give in to the DI's demands, so I told him I wasn't happy at all. I didn't like the thought, as I knew Jennifer wouldn't like either, of strangers rummaging through our personal things.

The DI, his eyes becoming a little more bulbous, his face a little deeper blue in colour, advised me that his request was perfectly normal procedure in cases such as this and if I refused his request he would return with a warrant to search the property.

I stared at him whilst weighing up the benefits of allowing the search now or refusing and see if he could return with a search warrant. All the time I felt his eyes moving over all my features, searching still for signs of my guilt. The DS and the two officers shuffled their feet on the doorsteps, expecting to move into action at any moment. The DI pressed his authority by explaining, with some menace in his voice.

"If I do have to return with a search warrant, it will be with a larger team of investigators and it will be considerably more thorough." I wasn't going to be bullied by this bastard, his attitude just made me stubborn and angry, so my reply wasn't created with a cool head.

"Are you suggesting that you have come here this morning, ill equipped and undermanned and unable to do a thorough search for Jennifer?" my voice went up to another level as I continued, "I think it would be in everyone's interest for you to organise your search team properly and if that takes a warrant, I suggest you go and get one before you return and start threatening me again."

"I assure you Mr Chambers, that we are trying to expedite our search for your wife, our enquiries are at an early stage and we are simply looking for clues to help with these enquiries," he explained with a more conciliatory tone. I sensed that he was not entirely confident with his position.

"If that's the case, why do you threaten me with search warrants and large teams of investigators if I don't allow you in. I'm sorry Detective Inspector, but I must ask you to leave, I intend making a complaint about your attitude, not just for this morning, but also last night, both my daughter and I were very distressed after your questioning. This is a very worrying time for us and we are extremely anxious about Jennifer's

169

whereabouts and we don't feel you are helping to find her."

"As you wish sir," was his reply and he and his 'troops' turned on their heels, returned to their cars and left, leaving me a little perplexed as to what would happen next. I was annoyed at myself, it would've been simpler just to have allowed them to search the house. I knew I'd been unreasonable and I felt the need to discuss it with someone, so I called Susanne.

She answered her phone immediately and I explained what had just happened.

"Dad, why didn't you just let them do their job, they're just trying to find mum," was her response, to which I needed to justify my actions.

"I know that, I should have let them in, it would have been so much simpler, it's just that bloody police officer, he irritates me so much and I don't know how searching the house was going to find Jennifer, he should be out tracing her movements and finding out where she is."

"I understand Dad, he is very annoying, but what do you think he'll do now? Do you think he will come back with a warrant and a full team of investigators?"

"I have absolutely no idea, but I'll let you know as soon as I hear from him again," was my reply.

I worried and fretted for the rest of the morning, admonishing myself for my stubborn attitude, wondering how long it would be before I heard further. As it happened, I didn't have to wait long. Just before lunchtime I answered a loud knocking on the front door. As I opened it DI Richards immediately announced.

"Mr Chambers, I have a warrant to search your premises and property and would ask you to step aside to allow these officers and technicians to enter, failure to do so could result in your arrest for obstruction. Do you have any question?" There was a short pause, before I recognised the futility of any further protest and stood aside to allow a sizeable team of uniformed and forensic personnel into the house. I could also see my car being placed on the back of a lorry.

"Where are you taking my car?" I demanded but was ignored. I was instructed to show them around the house and inform them of which bedroom was which. I then was sat at the kitchen table as technicians dusted for finger prints and tested surfaces for evidence of a crime. I was then led out to the garden to explain areas of newly cultivated soil, which I explained was Jennifer's domain and she had been preparing for the planting of a new rose bed. My explanations were received with questioning glances between the officers. As I returned to the kitchen the phone rang, it was Edith, who as usual didn't ask how I was, but immediately shouted.

"I've had the police at my door, what have you been doing? put Jennifer on."

"Susanne and I explained to you yesterday that Jennifer is missing, we don't know where she is, we've notified the police and that'll be the reason they've called to see you," I told her in a way that you address someone of low intelligence.

"I told them I was waiting for her to bring my lunch; do you know when she's coming? she's usually here by now and I've set the table."

"I don't know when she's coming, but when she does could you ask her to call me?" The call just ended as she hung up the phone. My God, I thought the fucking selfish, thoughtless cow has completely lost her marbles, fancy speaking to me like that when I'm worried to death about Jennifer's disappearance, I imagined the day when she wouldn't be able to call me again. Knowing that her calls would continue, irrespective of the situation going on around me, because she wanted her lunch, I called Susanne. The phone was again answered immediately, and I explained that the police had returned, with a warrant, and were currently searching the house so I couldn't speak for long but told her that Granny was waiting for her lunch. She begrudgingly agreed to take her a sandwich around, but making it sound as if I now owed her something.

The DI and DS Edwards suddenly appeared at my side, having now organised their troops they wanted to ask me some further questions, so we all shuffled back to the kitchen table, which had become one of the few places in the house that wasn't presently being checked for some evidence. As we sat down I couldn't help but admire the DS, she was so much more attractive than her superior, a full figure, pretty face, shining hair, but her eyes let her down badly, they behaved in exactly the same manner as the DI's, I really did feel as if I was 'under the spotlight' with both pairs of eyes searching for my guilt; I felt intimidated.

"Mr Chambers," began the DI, "I explained to you this morning that in these circumstances it is usual procedure for us to search the house of a missing person. This is not necessarily about you, we do not have any suspicions that any crime has occurred and therefore we do not suspect you or anyone else of causing your wife any harm, our concern is to look for evidence that may lead us to her whereabouts and ensure her safe return. We do however, need to rule out all possibilities. I hope this is clear." His official words of reassurance were undermined by the banging and clattering coming from all over the house as doors, cupboards, wardrobes and draws were opened and closed with very little care. I didn't comment so the DI opened his notebook and continued.

"When we spoke yesterday you told me that the last time you had seen your wife and the time you became concerned about her, a period of about twenty-four hours and I would like to go into a little more detail of this time." The questions started again, we went over everything, again, I had to even describe in more detail the television programmes we'd watched. He had already spoken to my neighbours, Valerie my secretary, one of my partners at work, he had even spoken to my client at Theale and it was the 'missing' time between the appointment ending and my return home that particularly interested him.

"You told me that after leaving your clients office at about three fifteen, your client has confirmed this, you went fishing for a couple of hours, can you give me details of that location. I opened the draw in a kitchen cupboard to retrieve the leaflet on the fishing lakes at Pangbourne and passed them to him. The noise and disturbance from around the house seemed to increase, as did my irritation so I decided that I should object further.

"DI Richards, I am feeling more and more threatened by your enquiries and actions, you have obviously spoken to my work colleagues, friends, neighbours and clients, goodness knows what they all must be thinking. You obviously believe I had something to do with Jennifer's disappearance and I'm beginning to think I need to consult a solicitor." The sound of breaking glass distracted me. "What the hell are those people doing, what do they expect to find?" I demanded loudly.

"They are simply doing their job looking for clues," explained the DS. "I'm afraid their work is going to take some time and it will probably later tomorrow before they finish. We would ask that you collect some of your possessions and leave the premises until further notice."

"Tomorrow, what the fucking hell are they going to doing that'll take until tomorrow," I shouted angrily.

CHAPTER 24

Basically, destroy my house and garden after four days of searching, was the conclusion by the time I was allowed back into the house.

Everything in my life had changed.

The police obviously believed me to be responsible for Jennifer's disappearance, and now the whole world had been given enough information by the media to ensure they believed I was guilty as well.

During the four days, the police activity had attracted the attention of the media, and on the second day a film crew had arrived, accompanied by a media helicopter that filmed events from the sky, broadcasting images of the house and garden, where a canvas canopy had been erected over Jennifer's rose bed and other parts of the garden to protect the excavations from the elements. Watching the broadcasts, I saw that our patio had also been taken up and was being excavated as well.

Nobody, apparently, had told the media anything, but they had nevertheless gained all the details of Jennifer's disappearance and the reasons for the search of the house and garden.

The media, in order to increase the drama and to keep their brainless audience interested, had changed the incident description from 'Missing Person' to 'Suspected Murder'. My description had also changed from 'Distraught Husband' to 'Suspected Killer', as my photo was displayed on the screen.

When the police 'circus' finally ended and departed empty handed, I was left stranded with a property that was uninhabitable and looked like a bomb site. I was still besieged by vultures from the press, who were eager to get at least a series of photographs, or better still, an interview with the 'Suspected Killer'. The police wanted the family to make a televised appeal, which was arranged and Susanne, David and myself all read out emotional statements asking for the public's help in finding our wonderful, loving and much missed mother and wife. I could feel the public's disbelief through the lenses of the cameras.

I had spoken with Susanne, David and several of my friends and colleagues, and none of them were now prepared to offer me accommodation or even come to pick me up. Every one of them had an excuse, the press intrusion being the most common, and within a very short period of time nobody would even answer my telephone calls.

The police and much of the media had now moved on to the tranquil fishing lakes at Pangbourne, where I had said I had gone after my meeting. I felt very guilty about inflicting the inflatable boats, divers, sniffer dogs and hordes of police on this beautiful environment but felt a real anger against the media for making everything so much worse.

CHAPTER 25

Diary note:

The 'Disappearance' is a good plan, but now having fully imagined the murder and all the consequences, would I kill Jennifer in this way? A difficult question. I'm sure the consequences wouldn't be as bad as I'd visualised them and I learnt a lot from my thoughts, so would deal with the situation a little differently. The whole plan certainly has potential.

Another realisation, as I completed my thoughts. After finally being told by the police that the case would remain on file as a missing person and not actively investigated further at this time, I realised the life insurances would not be paid out for seven years or until Jennifer's death was confirmed. That is disappointing.

The biggest downside however, would be that everyone would always suspect my guilt; my relationships with family, friends, neighbours, work colleagues and clients would never be the same and my life at home and at work would be over. No more invitations to golf days, lunches, seminars, dinner or even drinks after work, even strangers on the train would look at me trying to recall where they knew my face, before recollection dawned and they recognised me as that 'evil murderer'.

Already I now feel a growing enthusiasm for another plan, simply to kill Jennifer, but ensure that someone else gets the blame.

CHAPTER 26

Diary note:

Tuesday - At work, bit of a slow day. Feel OK, perhaps a little stressed and frustrated. Other than a lot of thinking and planning I haven't achieved much and life has just continued without any actual change. The time for action is becoming more and more urgent, I just need that little catalyst to give me a greater purpose and push me forward. Today I'm going to put down some of my thoughts for what I imagine could be the most challenging, but exciting of plans:

PLAN 3: - The 'Blameless' Murder.

Considered searching for a paid assassin but have decided the involvement of a 'third party' could lead to problems in the future. He could blackmail me forever or he may confess if he was careless and got arrested for the crime.

Considered who I should 'set up' as the murderer and have decided that it should be either my son, my son in law or my daughter. All of them are short of money, which could be used as a motive. My first choice would have been the evil bitch herself, Edith, but I cannot at the moment, imagine any realistic circumstance where I could implicate her.

Whoever is to be blamed, I would need to ensure that their fingerprints and DNA evidence were on the weapon, Jennifer and the surrounding surfaces. Jennifer's blood would have to be on their clothes and her valuables/money in their possession. Sounds quite difficult, particularly as I've got to actually kill her myself, but at the same time have a robust alibi and ensure that the person I am implicating doesn't have one. All sounds very complicated, need to give this a lot of thought.

Sitting back in my chair I look through the glass wall panelling to the activity in the office, everything looks and sounds normal, phones are ringing, computer screens flicker through pages of charts and data, keyboards are being tapped, tea and coffee being drunk, nobody even glances my way, but if I was to leave or was absent, everyone would see and know. Even when I go out to visit clients it's by appointment and there would only be a small window of time, but insufficient to go home, kill Jennifer before going to a scheduled meeting. So, as with my last plan, I would also need to take up cycling and fishing; both as an excuse to get out of the office.

The sounds of normality in the office are a reassurance and allow me to contemplate the many issues that surround a 'blame someone else' murder. I don't, after some careful consideration, feel it's right to blame a family member, they may be all arseholes, and even though the grandchildren are total little brats, I cannot allow them to be deprived of a parent and suffer the type of traumatic childhood that I had experienced, so it would have to be a stranger. I try to visualise a burglary gone wrong type of scenario, but getting witnesses, finger prints, DNA, and to be certain that they don't have an alibi, seems impossible, there are too many uncertainties and complications.

"Excusez-moi, Monsieur, voulez-vous une tasse de thé?" My reverie is interrupted by Valerie, who rarely volunteered to serve tea or coffee but had obviously been rehearsing this question and was anxious to practice her developing language skills, these skills certainly needed some refinement as her pronunciation still held her strong cockney accent. However, the vision of her standing in the doorway was more than sufficient compensation.

"Bien sûr, ce serait très gentil." I replied. My spoken French is not very good, but from the quizzical look on Valerie's face, my reply was obviously completely beyond her comprehension.

"Does that mean you do want a cup of tea?" she asked, laughing at her minor inadequacies.

"Yes please. Your French is coming along really well, are you having lessons?"

"No, I'm following a course on the internet, but it's not the same as talking with someone who can actually speak French, like you. Would you give me a French lesson?" Her question was delivered with a rather flirtatious glance that left me a little lost for words.

She smiled encouragingly, leaving me with several carnal thoughts, and completely distracted from the murderous plans I'd been contemplating. She soon returned with a cup, a small pastry and another smile.

"Merci beaucoup, mademoiselle."

"I love it when you speak French," she replied with a gravelly, mock French accent, and a flick of her hip, before leaving once again. I leant back in my chair, reviewing this interruption. It occurred to me that I had just missed out on an opportunity, Valerie could be my unwilling 'murderer'. In my mind I reran the last few minutes to consider how a different scenario could've unfolded:

"Excusez-moi, Monsieur, voulez-vous une tasse de thé?" My reverie is interrupted by Valerie who rarely volunteered to serve tea or coffee.

"Bien sûr, ce serait très gentil." I replied. My spoken French is not very good but from the quizzical look on Valerie's face my reply was obviously completely beyond her comprehension.

"Does that mean you do want a cup of tea?" she asked, laughing at her minor inadequacies.

"Yes please. Your French is coming along really well, are you having lessons?"

"No, I'm following a course on the internet, but it's not the same as talking with someone who can actually speak French, like you. Would you give me a French lesson?"

"I don't speak French very well myself, so it wouldn't be much of a 'French lesson', but I would love to help. As the French seem to spend most of their time eating and drinking, it would seem appropriate if we began by going to a restaurant."

"I would love that," Valerie agreed enthusiastically, "I'm always free after work."

"Well, what about this evening, I'm staying up in town tonight because of tomorrow's early morning conference calls."

"Perfect, are you sure? It must be a French restaurant so it's the right environment, should I find and book something?" her enthusiasm was very endearing, how could I resist granting this beautiful young woman's wishes.

"Excellent, I'll appreciate the company, I usually finish up having supper by myself when I stay over, so it'll be fun, I hope my French doesn't disappoint!"

As soon as Valerie left, I called Jennifer.

"Hello darling, how's your day?....."Good, good." Fuck there's never a short conversation with Jennifer and after 5 minutes listening for the umpteenth time about the problems at the church with the new flower arranging rota, I finally managed to interrupt.

"Listen darling, I'm so sorry to call so late in the day, but I'm going to have to work this evening and have some early morning calls to make, so I'm going to have to stay up here tonight.".….."Yes, I know, I'll miss my favourite liver and onions, but what can I do?"… "Yes, I'll see you tomorrow."….."Yes I love you too, Bye."…."Bye, yes, missing you as well, Bye… bye." Fucking hell, she's hard work.

I dialled my favourite hotel and booked a particularly special room, rather than the usual more spartan, 'corporate' room. You never know where these imaginings could end up! Time, in dreams has no relevance and Valerie soon returned to my office, now wearing a short black dress, her long legs balanced on seductively high heels, her golden hair was no longer tied back and flowed over her naked shoulders, her breasts were barely concealed by the very low-cut dress line, it was amazing how they were retained by

188

the soft material that allowed these magnificently curved mounds to move rhythmically as she walked. Her lips, painted with a bright red lipstick, spoke seductively.

"I'm ready whenever you are, I'm really hungry." So, we left.

We were seated in a secluded booth in the corner of a restaurant, the lighting subdued, and the table was lit by a candle whose flickering flame reflected an animalistic longing in Valerie's eyes. I had begun our French lesson, quite innocently, by telling her how to order a glass of wine, the words for salt and pepper, bread, water; and suddenly, it seemed, Valerie was almost fluent.

"What is the word for knee?" she asked as her soft, stockinged foot slid up my leg to my knee.

" Le Genou," I answered.

"And thigh?" her foot sliding higher up my leg.

"Cuisse."

"And here?" she whispered as her toes played over my crotch.

"Fourche," I also whispered in a slightly trembling voice, I felt beads of sweat on my face.

"And this very large, hard bit?"

"On l'appelle un grand, dur pine qui veut te baiser."

"I need you to translate that for me." Valerie asked innocently but seeming to already understand the meaning.

"It's a large hardon that wants to fuck you." I translated, just as the waiter served us with our 'entrée 'of Foie gras. He quickly left with his eyebrows raised.

"Tell me how you'd like to 'fuck me'."

"In French or English?" I asked, trying to force myself to eat something without choking!

"English, but with a French accent," she replied, her foot continuing its gentle motion.

"I would like to order soft deserts and take them back to the hotel room, strip you naked, tie you to the bed, serve the desert and eat it off 'tes seins', 'nombril' and 'ta chatte', licking every morsel thoroughly off 'ta clitoris'. I would then like to fuck you until orgasms rack your body with ecstasy. How about you, do you have any preferences?"

"That sounds divine to me," Valerie agreed, "I think I can certainly bring some interesting variations to your suggestion, but next time, when it's my turn to choose, I would like to suggest that we go 'Dogging', which is my favourite pastime."

"Dogging?" I asked, thinking perhaps we were going to involve pets or a kennel club outing. "What's 'Dogging'?

"It's where we invite a group of strangers to watch us having sex in a public place, I love it, it's so exhilarating, I love exposing myself and having people watch. Would you like to do that as well?

"Valerie, I'm really shocked, I never thought of you as an exhibitionist, but yes, I would be game to encourage your favourite pastime, but for now," turning to the waiter who had arrived to clear the table. "Can we order two large 'crème brulee' to take away.

Our hotel room was in complete disarray; the evening had been exactly as I'd visualised. Valerie and I awoke in a complete mess of sticky, caramelised custard, and smelling of sex, she turned to me.

"Philip, last night was everything I've dreamed of," she paused while I licked a piece sugar crystal off her beautiful rounded breast, her large pink nipple becoming immediately erect and her breathing deepening as her passion once again began to grow. "I have wanted to be with you ever since I started working for you, and my love for you has only deepened with desire. I want to be with you for always." My hunger for her body had been raised with the contact between my lips and her breast, my attention moved downward, until I was once again between her legs, the combination of her musky odour, the sharp salty taste of her orgasms and the sweet taste of custard, was overpowering as my lips drew her clitoris into my mouth. Her breath was rapid as she exclaimed.

"I love you Philip, please tell me you feel the same way?"

"I love you too, Valerie, you are the most beautiful women I have ever met," my voice was deep, and my words were muffled by the splendour of her 'chatte', she grasped my face and pulled me up, so she could kiss my lips.

"Please fuck me and tell me how much you love me" I thrust deep inside her, our rhythm became quick and hard, I repeated my love for her on every forward drive and we panted, "I love you," to each other, faster and faster until we were silenced as our bodies exploded in mutual orgasm.

As we lay back, still holding each other in a close embrace, I whispered.

"I do love you and want to be with you for always, but I'm married to Jennifer, she would never give me a divorce, I'm stuck, trapped in a loveless relationship that I cannot escape," my whisper became a sob, which made Valerie hold me in an even tighter embrace.

"We will be together, Philip, we belong in each other's arms, and I won't let that women ruin your life and keep us apart. Just love me and everything will work out perfect, believe in me, I'm your soulmate."

The days and weeks passed, Valerie and I took every opportunity to be together, our love and growing need to openly be a couple was frustrating, particularly for Valerie. She had become hugely jealous of Jennifer and her continuing role as my wife. One Monday morning on arrival at work, I was surprised to discover that Valerie wasn't at her desk. By 11.00am, and with her absence beginning to cause me concern, I called her mobile. It rang several times before it was answered by a gruff, male voice.

"Who's speaking?" it demanded.

"Er! I was trying to contact Valerie Aitchison, I'm sorry, I must have dialled the wrong number."

"No, this is the right number, who's speaking?" the gruff voice demanded again, with much more authority.

"This is Philip Chambers, I'm her employer. Is there a problem and who are you?" I asked with an equal level of authority.

"This is Detective Inspector Maigre, I'm afraid there's been an incident involving Miss Aitchison and your wife sir, I would ask that you come immediately to the station, we are trying to piece together the events leading to the incident and we require a statement from you quite urgently."

"What's happened?" I demanded, fear beginning to creep into my voice.

"We will be able to give you full details sir, at the station. Do you require me to send an officer to collect you?" the voice sounded a little threatening, so I refused his offer of 'transport' and confirmed that I would be at the station within an hour.

On the journey, I worried and fretted, trying to imagine what Valerie had done; had she killed Jennifer, but been caught in the act? Had Jennifer survived somehow and called the police? Had there been a fight between the two women and the neighbours called the police to break it up? Had Jennifer killed Valerie? My thoughts whirled around in my head.

DI Maigre, quickly bundled me into a claustrophobic interview room, which had that tired, stressed, sweaty smell. He never even offered me a cup tea, which I thought was mandatory in these circumstances, or any other pleasantries, before he snarled.

"Tell me about your relationship with Miss Aitchison."

"I think I deserve an explanation first as to what's happened and why you demanded that I come here so urgently to talk to you." The detective glowered at me and a tense silence lay heavy in the room.

"Mr Chambers, I'm sorry to inform you that your wife has been found dead at your home. We were called to the scene by a neighbour, a Mr Jeffries, who had gone to Miss Aitchison's assistance when her car wouldn't start and observed that she was covered in blood. On our arrival, we discovered that your wife had been struck with a blunt instrument, which we believe was a hammer found in Miss Aitchison possession. She has been arrested and is being held in custody. I understand this may be upsetting for you, but I need to understand your relationship with Miss Aitchison as she has suggested you may be complicit in your wife's death…….

"Philip, are you alright, you haven't drunk your tea?" Valerie asked, ending my dream.

"Yes, I'm fine, thank you, just resting my eyes and I forgot about the tea, any chance of a fresh one?"

"Bien sûr," she replied in her Cockney/French accent and strutted out.

CHAPTER 27

Diary note:

On the train going home, feeling very depressed. The daydream at the office had been fantastic and spectacularly real, but it's left me feeling very disappointed, recognising it could never happen, except in a dream. Worse still, because of its 'reality', it took me a while to realise that I wasn't going for a wonderful evening out with Valerie, but would be travelling home to Slough to enjoy liver and onions with Jennifer.

I have made up my mind, I'm not going to have any more frivolous thoughts about killing Jennifer, from this moment on I'm going to focus on serious plans, thoughts and real actions. I realise I can only do this by myself, involving others is too unpredictable and risky. So back to PLAN 3 – The 'Blameless' murder, I have a quite bizarre idea to work on.

Tuesday bedtime – Just endured the dreaded liver for dinner, didn't even have the assistance of my son this week to help dispose of it, in fact, I think Jennifer cooked more of it in case he or another visitor unexpectedly arrived. Giving lots of thought to my new plan, which has raised my spirits a little.

CHAPTER 28

I need to watch and observe Jennifer's daily routines to see where an opportunity may exist. I've always believed that her days and weeks were very routine. As well as her involvement with the church and her fund-raising activities, she also helps organise and deliver lunches on a Monday, Wednesday and Fridays to the frail and elderly with Meals on Wheels. Apart from these charitable services, her time, I think, seemed to be spent shopping or at the house cooking, cleaning and working in the garden. But I couldn't be certain and need to follow and monitor her daily life.

The idea that I'm planning, at first seemed completely ridiculous, and very risky, but the more I've thought about it, the more I feel enthused by the challenge and its potential for success. I will need a disguise that will allow me to be readily accepted into people's homes, I have thought and dismissed the obvious of dressing as a policeman, doctor, fireman, which will raise questions and will be remembered. My other more likely disguises are a social worker or a vicar.

A social worker would require some form of identification and could meet with resistance and suspicion, a vicar however, only requires a 'Dog Collar' as a means of identity. A man of God is usually trusted, and even when it's not a vicar they recognise, it's accepted that they may be visiting a parish or standing in for their usual vicar while he's away.

My thoughts begin with the Reverend Whitehead, our own vicar, and in fact, the many other vicars I have encountered. Their dress code, when not performing religious ceremonies, is quite simple and plain; a dark suit, a grey or black collarless style shirt and their 'dog collar', appear to be their 'off duty' uniform, enhanced by the badge of honour, a crucifix. Vicars by their nature and occupation do not attract attention, they are believed by the majority to be harmless, caring individuals, to be avoided at all costs for fear they may start bothering you with 'God stuff'. They are never viewed suspiciously and can often gain access to places without question. Gone are the religious zealots from my Presbyterian childhood, all seems now to have been replaced with this bland stereo type. If I was to become disguised as a vicar, I should immediately gain the same status, theoretically.

Another key feature of a vicar is his mode of transport; a car has obviously now become the norm, but riding a bicycle is still not unusual, and even if this attracted some attention, people would only remember seeing a vicar on a bike. A bike does not have any means of identification other than being silver or blue and is therefore untraceable.

I'm going to concentrate on Jennifer's Meals on Wheels delivery days. Once I've established her routines by following her; observing which houses she regularly visits, the times of her arrival and departure, whether she's alone on her Monday, Wednesday and Friday service, I would be able to establish when and where to carry out her demise.

CHAPTER 29

Diary note:

Wednesday - Fucking Macaroni and Cheese, again!

Jennifer was a little upset and angry tonight, seemingly the vicar's wife has reorganised for a second time the church flower arranging duties, to allow for other volunteers to have a turn. This has caused some further issues as Jennifer has lost one of her prestigious 'slots'. I did try to listen to her in order to gain some insights, but it's not easy. Got to see very little television while she ranted on for what see like hours; it's a relief to go to bed.

Need to record the outline of my new plan and detail those elements that require investigation, experimentation and procurement. The plan, in simple outline, is to disguise myself as a vicar, enter a house of an elderly person who is waiting for her Meals on Wheels lunch to be served by Jennifer, and when she arrives, kill her before disappearing.

To begin I need much more information on Meals on Wheels, particularly Jennifer's routine, I need a vicar's disguise, a bicycle both for my 'out of office' cycling excuse and as part of the vicar disguise.

Diary note:

It's been a busy few days and my determination to progress with actions rather than pure imaginings has me very excited, although in quieter moment of reflexion, feelings of anxiety still haunt me. But my determination is growing. I have bought a bike and some fishing tackle and told Valerie of my future intensions to be away from the office occasionally pursuing my new hobbies.

It's now Sunday afternoon. After the family had left and all the debris had been cleared away, I told Jennifer I was going to have a rest after such a delicious lunch. I know this was a lie, but it was the only excuse I could think of to lock myself up in the bedroom, dress up as a vicar and practice in front of the mirror. I managed to buy everything over the past few days but now realise I forgot to buy a bible.

I definitely look like a vicar but feel a little nervous going out in public, which I intend to do tomorrow.

―――――――

I leave for work on Monday morning, same time, same routine, but as I arrive at the station I immediately enter the toilets and change into my vicar's outfit, which I have carefully packed into my briefcase. The full vicar disguise includes; thick rimmed glasses, a subtle hair piece, a cap, plain glasses with brown frames, a grey mackintosh coat and most importantly, black leather gloves. On exiting the toilet cubicle and examining myself in front of the mirror, I am again pleased with the disguise, and am encourage when another man enters, greets me with a simple "Morning Vicar" before standing at a urinal, quite unaware of the deception.

I take my bike, which I have chained in the stand at the side of the station, and feeling very self-conscious, set off into the streets of Slough to see how people perceive my new persona. I am gratified and surprised that no one seems to give me a second glance and as I suspected, everyone is anxious to avoid any embarrassing contact with anything to do with the church and religion. As my confidence increases and having cycled the parts of Jennifer's Meals on Wheels route I have managed to learn from her, even passing our own and Edith's house, I decided to test my disguise by doing some shopping.

The first was a corner shop run by an Indian family, who addressed me as 'Father' and almost bowed in reverence as I bought a box of Mr Kipling's Angel Cakes - my favourites. It was when I visited other shops that I began to recognise a pattern to the average person's reaction to a 'man of the cloth'; they seem unsure of what title to use in address, varying from "Vicar" or "Father" to one young shop assistant who called me "Your Holiness". The other thing

I observed, was there was never any eye contact, they seemed to see only the 'dog collar' and their mind filled in the blanks.

I felt much more confident, my only concerns being was if I met an actual vicar. I had rehearsed a simple story, that I was down from the Midlands, where my Parish was located, visiting an old university friend, but I did worry in case this real vicar may start asking questions that I would struggle to answer.

As late morning approached, I set off on my quest to follow Jennifer. As she left our house and drove directly to the Meals on Wheels depot, it was sometimes difficult to keep up with her and my fitness, or lack of it, had me gasping for breath and my legs aching; already my backside had gone numb. Fortunately, I always managed to catch her up at traffic lights. Finally, I arrived at the depot and sat on a bench close by, soon observing Jennifer, together with several other late-middle-aged women, moving in and out of the building with boxes. Their appearance seemed to define who they were and what they did – stout frame, greying hair, plain, traditional dress and sensible shoes; formidable and practical women who would certainly challenge my disguise if I got too close.

There was a familiar smell in the air that for some reason I found quite unpleasant and couldn't quite identify. I watched as cars and vans were quickly loaded up and began to leave, I was caught by surprise when I saw Jennifer sitting as a passenger in a small white van with SLOUGH COMMUNITY SERVICES printed on the door panel go by. Once again, I had to start peddling hard to keep up, nearly losing sight several times, before following it down an estate road, where it stopped and both Jennifer and the driver got out, opened the rear doors and took out a small, white polystyrene box each. Jennifer went to number 32 on the left-hand side of the street and the driver went into number 37 on the right. I noticed that they both entered without knocking or being invited, they were obviously expected. I also noted the time of their arrival and how long before they left the house, which was just under 7 minutes for both of them. The van then moved further down the street and the procedure was repeated at numbers 48 and 53, again they were in the house for 7 minutes.

The van continued it circuitous route, up and down streets. Finally, having delivered all of their stock they left, obviously to return to the depot and reload. I felt I couldn't do any more chasing and following for today and decided to return to the station, park the bike, get changed and go into the office. However, as I approached the station, the van with Jennifer in it passed me before being held up at the traffic lights. I couldn't resist and decided to follow her. I was most surprised when it turned into Sycamore Close, more fondly known to me as Coven Street as it was where Edith lived, and it was outside her house that the van stopped. Again, the two ladies exited the van, collected a box each, the driver crossing the street to make her delivery and Jennifer went into the evil bitch herself's house. Now this was a surprise.

The driver returned to the van first and drove a little farther down the road to make further deliveries, before turning around and driving back to collect Jennifer, who had now left her mother's house. I continued to follow the van, again up and down streets making deliveries, before turning into our road and stopping outside our house. Only Jennifer got out, opened the rear door and removed two white boxes and took them into our house. A couple of minutes later Jennifer returned, still carrying the two boxes, which she put in the back before driving off in the van. Now this was a surprise and I was very curious, although a sinking realisation was beginning to dawn in my mind.

Returning once again to the station, I secured the bike, changed in the gent's toilet and walked back home in my suit. Mr Jeffries was outside brushing his already immaculate drive and waving his hand he shouted.

"Hello Phillip, you've just missed Jennifer, she left 20 minutes ago."

"Hello Mr Jeffries, no problem, I didn't expect her to be home, she does her Meals on Wheels round on a Monday. I've just come to pick up some papers before I go to visit a client. I'm then going for a fly fishing lesson, I'm taking up trout fishing." I replied.

"Fishing, I never thought of you as a fisherman, but I'm always happy to share your catch." He chuckled.

"I think it'll be a little while before I'm likely to catch anything, but if I do, you'll be the first to know!" I walked off, leaving Mr Jeffries to his everlasting chores and I entered our house. Everything was still, quiet and 'normal', but I felt anxious, not really wanting to confirm my growing suspicions. I walked slowly down the hall and opened the kitchen door, my eyes immediately settling on the two aluminium foil trays resting on the drainer. I walked over and touched them, they were still hot and as I carefully folded back the cover of one, the smell assaulted my nostrils; everything seemed to freeze as thoughts and emotions flooded through me. Extreme sadness and a sense of betrayal being the most powerful.

How could she? All these years of being a dutiful husband, never straying, being unfaithful or abusing our vows and promises to each other, always treating her with respect, always supporting her in every way. Everything had just been false, our lives together had been false, she had constantly deceived me.

My feelings of sadness increased as I thought of George. Had he known that he was also being deceived and betrayed by Edith for all those years, that poor gentle man who always tried his best to help and care for everyone. Tears slid down my face as I felt both his, and my own unhappiness shudder through me. I felt hollow.

I couldn't take my eyes off these symbols of betrayal, the more I looked, the more I felt all my emotions being replaced by a cold vengeful anger. My immediate reaction was to kill both Jennifer and her evil mother and to hell with the consequences. The thought that I could be at Edith's house in 5 minutes, with my hands around her throat, choking her to death, knowing that her last meal was that evil Shepherd's Pie. I could be back inside 10 minutes, plenty of time before Jennifer would return and I could repeat the same fate on her. But my head soon took control over my heart, I knew the plan I was already enacting would give me much more satisfaction and a lifetime to enjoy their deaths. Their deaths had instantly become a priority in my life and any doubts I may have held had completely gone. No more 'Planning and Researching', I had embarked on this Plan and intended to execute it, regardless of the consequences.

I resealed the evil supper, collected my things, returned to the station, took the first train and went into the office.

"I thought you were having a day of cycling and fishing," demanded Valerie.

"I was, but a few personal issues cropped up, so I'll make it another day. Anything needing my attention?"

"Yes, quite a few phone calls, I've left notes on your desk, and Mr Green from Scotmill in Theale wants you to arrange another appointment, his policies are coming up for renewal and he wants you to visit him."

"Ok, thanks, I'll do that," and shut my office door behind me.

CHAPTER 30

Diary note:

Monday afternoon.

Just shut myself away in the office, I need to escape from everyone and everything, this is now my 'safe' place. I am so angry and upset. I still find it hard to accept that Jennifer has deceived me all our married life; how could she do that? how could she serve me the tasteless Meals on Wheels shit every day for all these years? She obviously doesn't love or care for me as I've loved and cared for her. I loathe and detest her so much at this moment, her deceit has made a complete mockery of our lives together. Has everything in our married life been false?

Despite all my emotional feelings, I want to remain very calm and focused; there can be no mistakes. I am ready to continue with this plan, but now for real. I just need to consider a few concerns.

My new 'persona' as a vicar is very good and working well, before I became distracted, so I intend to use the knowledge I have, and visit some of the people that were served meals on wheels by Jennifer. I can then select one individual whose house has the best situation and escape route.

There is one problem however with this direct approach that I need to address for my own 'safety'. If I was to select this one house and kill Jennifer, suspicion could be focussed on me. Unfortunately therefore, Jennifer cannot be the first victim, the event must appear to be that of 'serial killer'. Therefore, the first murder, and probably a second, would best be in different service areas of Meals on Wheels to distract the investigators.

I believe this is generally a good plan. My cautious approach to Jennifer's murder will require a lot of effort, information gathering and cycling in my vicar's outfit, all of which will be worth it. If I plan and arrange everything perfectly it will allow me to kill both Jennifer and Edith at the same time. I will have to improve my appearance greatly to prevent them from recognising me, but I'm sure I can get some guidance off the internet.

I have given some thought as to the murder weapon and am going to use a hammer as 'Valerie's' had in my 'dream' from the other day.

When I go home I'm not going to change my routine or my attitude or relationship with Jennifer, despite a strong desire to quiz her over 'Her' recipe for the Shepherd's Pie and all the other crap she's been feeding me.

This has been a long, stressful and emotional day.

CHAPTER 31

Diary note:

Sunday.

Continuing to suppress the feelings of anger and betrayal.

Another fine lunch with the family. Suzanne 'borrowed' some more money as the new car needed taxed and insured. I questioned this as I couldn't understand how it was some sort of surprise. I didn't receive any answer, only glowering looks. The brats broke the glass panel of the back door, 'by accident', I'm not sure throwing a cricket ball across the kitchen, unfortunately narrowly missing Jennifer's head, could be classed as an 'accident', but apparently these things happen.

Plans progressing well, I'm targeting Windsor and Maidenhead Meals on Wheels.

CHAPTER 32

The staff and particularly Valerie seem to accept my greater absence from the office and I'm getting much fitter from all the cycling. I've become quite proficient at fishing and have caught a number of trout, I fulfilled my promise to Mr Jeffries and presented him with a sizeable fish that his wife cooked and served to Jennifer and me for supper one night at their house. I think this was the first time we've been invited to any of our neighbours. Jennifer didn't eat any of the trout, which I thought was delicious, claiming that she disliked freshwater fish and asked if she could have some tinned tuna on the side instead. I don't bring any of my catches home anymore as she refuses to cook them, preferring instead to put them in the bin. This suits me fine as I don't have to produce anything to prove I've been fishing.

I've also now become very confident dressing up as a vicar and cycling around Maidenhead and Windsor. I've followed and recorded two women, both so like Jennifer. Dressed as a vicar, I have on many occasions now, simply walked into different houses about 30 minutes before the arrival of the lunch deliveries, and introduced myself as the Reverend Martin Entwistle,

Having done simple searches through the public records of the Local Authority Rating Department, accessing the names of the occupiers was easy. I did this so as I entered the house I could call out their name, which immediately seemed to reassure them, particularly when they saw 'the dog collar'. Of these properties many weren't suitable for a variety of reason: the occupier told me to leave immediately or they were only physically infirm and their sharp minds and eyesight would remember and recall my visit in detail, or the rear access was not suitable to enable my escape. However, the principal reason for me not selecting several of the houses was that I would not have been able to kill the Meals on Wheels person as they were too nice, even though they served the same dreadful food, they were forgiven for their gentle and caring kindness.

I have now selected four target households. Two to action over the next few weeks and two I will keep in reserve in case I am unable to proceed with either of the first two for any reason, or the police don't make a connection to Meals on Wheels and I have to 'do' a third; this is important to shift any focus on me before I end Jennifer and her evil mother's existence.

The first of my selection was Mr Smails, he wanted to talk and talk, whilst showing me pictures of his family, repeating constantly the same stories in a 'memory loop'. When the Meals on Wheels lady, who hardly seemed to notice me as she efficiently bullied and rushed poor Mr Smails into washing his hands, sitting him at the table, cruelly forcing the napkin between the loose skin of his neck and the tight collar of his shirt, before firmly placing his plate of food in front of him and commanding him to,

"Eat," and Mr Smails endeavoured to oblige.

I felt like gagging for him when I saw (and smelt) that it was liver and onions and wondered if Meals on Wheels nationally only served the same menu. Did they buy up all the toughest of meats in bulk from abattoirs in Eastern Europe, before distributing it throughout the country to these poor defenceless souls, whose only crime was that they had become elderly or infirm and struggled to look after themselves. Poor old buggers. The only difference between this liver and onions and the Slough liver and onions is that it's Wednesday, and I get served it on a Tuesday, as I've recently discovered.

The efficient woman fussed about for another minute before collecting up what I assumed were yesterday's plates and gruffly shouted,

"See you tomorrow," before striding out the front door, banging it loudly as she went, making Mr Smails jump nervously. Never once did she acknowledge my presence, ask who I was or what I was doing there, she obviously wanted to complete, as quickly as possible, her charitable duties and return home to feed her poor, unsuspecting husband some of this abominable, liverish mess. This bitch deserved to be hit with a hammer, so it was an easy choice to put a red star against Mr Smails's house.

My second selection is an elderly lady called Mrs Porter, she was thrilled to see me and treated me like we had known each other for years and wanted to hold my hand while we spoke. She told me that she had been out shopping earlier and bought some gin and would I mind pouring her a glass and of course, one for myself, very kind I thought. There was no gin, so I poured her some lemonade and she seemed quite happy. Her lunch of Meat Loaf with a potato crust and vegetables, smelt the same as Shepherd's Pie and I wondered if the cook had added too much cornflour, making the mince too thick and decided to slice it up and call it meat loaf. Mrs

Porter showed little interest in it preferring to continue drinking her 'gin'.

My third choice was a Mrs Carter who wanted to know how my family was and I began telling her about how my daughter had just bought a car, "A car you say, do you hear that Gerald, the vicar's daughters bought a car," she spoke to 'someone' who was seemingly sitting beside her, "how would I know?" she continued, "I don't know anything about cars, ask him yourself." She turned to face me, obviously waiting for me to continue the conversation with 'Gerald', who I assumed was her husband.

"It's red Vauxhall Corsa," I replied, not sure how this conversation would progress as the moment stretched out in silence.

"Gerald doesn't think they're very good cars," Mrs Carter finally announced, nodding her head in apparent agreement with her husband. "Do you have a car vicar?"

"Yes I do," I replied, "I have a silver, Bentley Convertible." Again, a long moment stretched out in silence before she spoke again.

"Gerald doesn't think they're very good cars," again nodding her head in agreement. This odd conversation was brought to a halt with the arrival of lunch. Macaroni and Cheese, and it was Wednesday, so felt completely 'normal' to me.

My final choice was a Mrs Pomphrey who immediately asked me as I entered, if I was there to take her away. "Take you away where?" I asked foolishly, and a 'Catholic' Heaven and Hell discussion followed that ended by her insisting I give her Holy Communion and read her Last Rites. Thankfully we were disturbed at this moment by the Meals on Wheels 'Carer'. I immediately knew it was Friday because it was fish. My God, it looked and smelt terrible, I felt it was this meal that deserved 'Last Rites'.

All these three elderly ladies had their lunches served to them in a similar uncaring, disinterested fashion as Mr Smails had been. All of them were lovely people, I just felt so heart sorry for their situation and continuing abuse with these appalling 'last suppers' served to them in the twilight of their lives.

CHAPTER 33

It was a Wednesday morning when I left the office, taking the train to Maidenhead and changing into my vicar's outfit in the toilet, which wasn't very easy; the carriage rocked and swayed as the train sped along. Nobody seemed to notice that a businessman had entered the toilet, but a vicar had emerged. I returned to a different seat in a different carriage however, to avoid any possibility of confusion. Nobody took any notice of me.

Leaving Maidenhead station on my bike, which I'd brought over yesterday evening and securely chained up. I cycled directly to the rear of Mr Smails's house, pushing it up the short path and leaning it against the wall of the house beside his entrance door. Glancing further along the side of the house to the front of the building and the estate road, I couldn't see anyone, so entered, calling to Mr Smails as I shut the door. I felt very nervous and could hardly stop shaking as I sat down in the chair opposite Mr Smails who immediately started talking, telling me the same stories that he'd told on my first visit. He was about to get out the photo albums when Mrs Efficiency arrived with his lunch, following her same routine of bullying and organising him. Finally, she went through to the kitchen.

"Excuse me Mr Smails," I said, standing up and quietly going through to the kitchen myself. The woman stood facing the kitchen unit with her back to me, busily scraping the last morsel of potato from the container onto a plate. The smell spurred me on and without any hesitation I removed the hammer from under my coat, took firm hold and brought it down it a hard-swinging blow directly on the crown of her head. Her legs collapsed immediately, and she fell to the ground almost soundlessly. Again, without any delay, I brought the hammer down, this time connecting with her forehead, the head of the weapon embedding itself deeply; skin, bone, gristle and brain offering very little resistance to its passage.

Carefully putting the hammer into a sealed polythene bag and back into my coat pocket, I walked out the back door, but couldn't resist glancing back to observe the still twitching and bleeding corpse; incredibly the woman still held onto the tin tray as if, even in death, she couldn't end her routine of trying to serve up the toxic meal. I quickly walked down the little rear path with my bike and cycled back to the railway station. My only thought was for Mr Smails, who I knew would be still sitting at his dining table, his napkin wedged into his collar waiting for his lunch. As it was the dreaded Shepherd's Pie, I consoled myself that I had probably done him a favour.

CHAPTER 34

Diary note:

Wednesday evening.

Macaroni and cheese bake for me tonight. Joy! However, I would've struggled to eat anything, no matter what was served, as my anxiety and nerves continue to knot in my stomach.

After leaving Maidenhead, changing on the train, trying to clean off the few small blood splatters off my coat, which I've since decided to throw away and replace, I spent the rest of the afternoon in the office reading reports and replying to phone messages. Valerie kindly kept bringing cups of tea, fortunately her attempts at speaking French have stopped.

Jennifer and I watched the news together and a suspicious death was reported at the house of an elderly man in Maidenhead, it gave no details other than that the police were investigating. I will follow these investigations closely over the next couple of weeks, before I attempt my next visit to Mrs Porter.

Going fishing tomorrow, it'll give me a chance to collect my bike from Maidenhead station and have some peaceful relaxation to settle my nerves.

CHAPTER 35

Diary note:

10 days since my last entry, feeling very positive. Nothing has happened, there's been very little news reports on the murder other than that the police continue to issue statements confirming that 'investigations are continuing'. The press seems to have lost interest and moved on to new headline stories.

I have revisited, in my mind, that lunchtime at Mr Smails's house and have repeatedly watched myself bringing down the hammer; the image as it hit the back of Mrs Gladstone's head - I discovered her name from the newspaper when it was released - watching in slow-motion as the hammer touched her hair, her skin and entered the skull in a blur, the speed with which she fell to the ground, twitching and writhing; my slight confusion that caused me to hit her a second time on the forehead believing she may have survive the first blow. Despite this crushing second impact and the deep penetration of the hammer, she still continued to twitch. I have subsequently discovered that this is 'normal' in a body immediately after death. Although I won't worry so much in future, I will always apply this second blow, just to be sure and to show continuity of method to the police.

Jennifer hasn't said very much, other than it was probably Mr Smails himself that killed Mrs Gladstone, explaining that from her experience, these elderly, housebound invalids, could often become aggressive and deranged as their dementia prevented them from remembering who people were. Jennifer's such an expert.

I am now filled with confidence and fully energised for my visit to Mrs Porter on Tuesday. I constantly remind myself that no two visits will be the same and to prepare myself for the unexpected. I do however, intend to follow exactly the same plan, I think keeping it simple and without any elaboration or additional drama is most important. I just hope that after this second killing the police or the press will make a connection with Meals on Wheels rather than simply 'The Carer' that had been used to describe Mrs Gladstone. If they don't my next visit, following Mrs Porter, will be to Mrs Carter.

CHAPTER 36

Diary note:
Tuesday night.

I'm good at this. After a conversation with Mrs Porter, and 'Gerald', who continued, according to Mrs Porter to dislike everything and anything I told her, the Meals on Wheels 'carer' arrived. I'm pleased because the 'procedure' was most successful and almost a repeat of the event in Mr Smails's house. One very enlightening difference however, I only hit the carer once on the back of the head, again she fell instantly to the floor, but this time the hammer had become jammed, and as she lay twitching on the floor and I twisted and pulled on the hammer I felt an energy pass through my hands, which I somehow sensed was her life force leaving her body. As I become more experienced, I'm sure I will learn to be more aware of this sensation.

Jennifer's mother, Edith, has not been well today; her varicose veins have caused her legs to swell and become extremely painful, I felt it was my duty to call by to see her on my way home. I don't think the day could have ended any better, between seeing Edith in pain and then going to the Chinese Cookhouse for a takeaway supper; Jennifer was unable to serve her usual liver and onions because she had to nurse her mother and therefore had been unable to do her Meals on Wheels duty. Perfect, all is going well.

CHAPTER 37

The office had been very busy this morning, the phone had never stopped, and they'd been a number of staff meetings to attend; we are about to start a recruitment campaign as the business continues to expand. By the time a working lunch had passed, everything began to quieten, as it usually did on a Friday.

As I sat at my desk reviewing papers and signing off different consents, my mind began to drift to my next, and final murders, that of Jennifer and Edith, which I planned for Monday lunchtime, everything was arranged. With the killing of Mrs Fletcher at Mrs Porter's house, the press had linked the fact that both Mrs Fletcher and Mrs Gladstone had both been serving lunches with Meals on Wheels. The police, who seemingly had no clues, continued to issue statements confirming that 'investigations are still continuing'. The press however, were announcing to the world that a serial killer may be targeting these kind, gentle and caring people, their headlines now reported the murderer as 'The Trolley Dolly Killer'.

I had worried that killing Jennifer and Edith at the same time may be quite difficult, as even with my disguise I suspected that either of them, or probably both, would see through my vicar's outfit. Fortunately, Edith's varicose veins had become serious last week and had, only this morning, some veins removed from both her legs, so apart from light exercise she was going to be house bound, in a chair or bed, for the next couple of weeks.

I had visualized and rehearsed, in my mind, many scenario's of how events would unfold on Monday and once again my thoughts drifted to my arrival at Sycamore Close. I had made special efforts with my facial disguise, adding a moustache and a different hat. As expected the front door was locked, but I entered quickly and quietly using my own key, fixing back the sneck so it remained unlocked when it shut. I stood absolutely still, listening for a sound that would identify Edith's location in the house, the minutes tick by before I heard from upstairs the sound of her clearing her throat.

Climbing the stairs, trying to avoid any creaks by only treading on the side, I slowly made my way up, constantly listening for any sounds. At the top I moved across the landing, again pausing, this time outside the bathroom door, I could only hear the sound of pages being turned in a magazine. I advance to the bedroom door, I knew she wouldn't be able to see me because her bed was against the wall behind the door. I glance through the small crack between the door and the frame and can see the bed with a large mound at the base where a frame has been installed to take the weight off her legs, I can also see the magazine and her hands, but her head and shoulders are obscured. I want this to be a complete surprise and as much as I would have preferred to hurt and torture her over a long period of time, I raise the hammer, walk around the door and hit her straight in the eye socket; I was aiming for her forehead, but she had begun to turn her head as the blow struck. I had expected her to fight back if I didn't kill her with the first blow and she instantly began to wail, her arms whirling defensively. The second blow with the hammer smashed her arm, shards of skin and bone erupted across the bedlinen, her movements slowed, and her wails became a whimpering groan as the hammer arrived for the third time, and with much force it found its original target and finally, other than the normal twitching, she remained still. I immediately released the hammer leaving it wedged in her head, I did not want to feel the passage of this evil bitch's life force.

When all was again still, I recovered the hammer, wiping it on the bedsheets, sealed it in a polythene bag and put it back in my coat pocket. I then withdrew a second hammer, I didn't want to use the same hammer as forensics may establish from the cross contamination that Edith had been killed first, I wanted to leave as much confusion as possible to the sequence of events.

I remained standing behind the bedroom door on Edith's side, waiting and listening for Jennifer's arrival. The minutes ticked by slowly, I heard a car outside, doors opening and closing, voices, the front door opened, and Jennifer shouted.

"Hello," and when she received no reply repeated her greeting. I heard her go through to the kitchen before exploring the rest of the ground floor. Still not finding her mother, Jennifer began to climb the stairs.

"Hello Mum, are you asleep?" she shouted. I waited, silently as I listened to her walk across the landing and into the bedroom. I don't think she even saw me before the hammer hit her directly on the top of her head. Like Mrs Fletcher and Mrs Gregory, Jennifer went down like a stone. With the hammer raised, I bent over her, stared into her flickering eyes, I knew she could see me, and told her firmly,

"I hate Shepherd's Fucking Pie you Lying Fucking Bitch." A confused look seemed to appear briefly in her eyes before the hammer made its final decent.

I was free, justice had been served and a feeling of euphoria raced through my veins, but the feeling was disturbed by the telephone ringing on my desk.

"Yes Valerie?" I asked, trying to sound authoritative but actually sounded irritable, as I was due to the interruption to my imaginings at the best moment.

"Mr Chambers, there are two police officers asking to see you."

"Police officers?" I repeated.

"Yes, police officers," repeated Valerie, "do you want me to show them in, they say it is extremely urgent?"

"Yes of course," I instructed, putting down the phone.

My mind went into overdrive. Had they found my diary? – No, it was here with me in my briefcase. Had they found some forensic evidence at Mr Smails's or Mrs Porter's houses?

– No, surely not, I had been most careful, and the police don't have any records of my DNA, I've never been in contact with the police for decades. Had I been spotted and identified on CCTV cameras at the station or on the train? – That was always a possibility that couldn't be avoided. Valerie entered the office and stood back to allow the officers to enter before reluctantly leaving with a curious look back at me as she shut the door.

"Mr Philip Chambers?" the male officer asked, I nodded. "I'm Detective Inspector Ross and this is Constable Downie from Slough Constabulary." 'Shit', I thought, these are real policeman, not Inspector Tracey, Dixon, Richards or Maigre from my imaginings.

"Would you like to sit down sir, I have some rather upsetting news." I sat back down at my desk with a defeated slump. "I'm sorry to inform you but your wife has been involved in a road accident, she was taken to Wexham Park Hospital, but I'm sorry to advise you that she was pronounced dead on arrival. I am terribly sorry for your loss."

I felt very confused and lost for words, only minutes before, in my mind, I had been hitting Jennifer over the head with a hammer. The officers mistook my inability to respond as shock.

"What road accident?" I illogically asked, not winning any BAFTA this time as no play acting was necessary.

"We are still investigating the incident Mr Chambers, but a colleague of hers reported that while they were delivering Meals on Wheels lunches, your wife inadvertently stepped out in the road and was hit by a passing vehicle. An ambulance was immediately called, and the paramedics did all they could at the scene. Mr Chambers, is there anyone you wish us to contact immediately?"

"No," I replied, "I think it's best that I tell the family."

"In that case sir, can we take you to the hospital? We have a car outside, I'm afraid we must ask you to come with us to identify your wife" Again, I simply nodded, what else was there to say, I couldn't work out how I felt.

CHAPTER 38

It was a grey, misty damp day as we all stood mournfully around the newly dug grave, the coffin rested on its wooden supports ready to be lifted and lowered into its permanent resting place in the dank cold earth. A depressed silence enveloped all those who stood around, a coldness crept into everyone's soul, it was a joyless morning, made even more joyless at the sight of Jennifer's 'friends' from the church and Meals on Wheels, who grouped together like a pack of dogs. They seemed to be all clones of Jennifer, robust women in tweedy coats, skirts and hats, all with sensible shoes, all with a passion to ensure that life would continue in a rigid, routine way; Their Way, because Their Way was the Right Way and any other Way would be foolish.

After I had identified Jennifer's body at the morgue, a sight that had reduced me to tears, seeing her lying there, so at peace, so innocent, her face relaxed; I could only see the young Jennifer that I met on Brighton Pier all those years ago. How could this have happened? How could our love for each other be extinguished so abruptly? This was not my plan; it was my responsibility to punish her with death for the misery she had brought into my life. How could a random car travelling too fast, at a rare moment when Jennifer was distracted, meet in destiny? Are our lives and deaths preordained in some way? Everything suddenly seemed so pointless.

The family were shocked, as I was, even Edith's evil little eyes manage to reluctantly squeeze out a tear when she was told; this was however, a short-lived moment of emotion as within less than 20 minutes she was asking me what arrangements I would be making for her continuing care, in particular, who would be bringing her something to eat as she was very hungry due to Jennifer's failure to deliver her lunch? I just left, this woman will need to be dealt with.

The family's shock and distress also didn't seem to last long before 'sensitive' enquiries were being made about potential inheritances; "Will you be selling the house?", "How will Mum's affairs be managed?", "Can I borrow Mums car." What they all really wanted to ask was, "When is the Will being read and how much do you think we'll all get?" I felt quite hurt by their greedy, thoughtless, selfishness, but consoled myself in the knowledge that I knew the contents of Jennifer's will and everything was left to me.

And now here we all stood around the grave, waiting for the Reverend Whitehead to appear from the church. His sermon had been one of genuine sorrow, praising Jennifer for her dedication to the church and the community. When I spoke, I repeated much of his praise, but also expressed my own grief at how Jennifer had been so suddenly taken out of our lives and how my heart ached with sorrow at the thought of not having a last treasured moment with her. I allowed a lengthy pause to allow emotions to flow through the mourners.

However, I felt a little cheered, as I continued to say a few further words on behalf of Jennifer's mother Edith, who unfortunately couldn't be at the service due to her continuing problems with her health. After the service I had to explain to several people that following the operation on her legs, several complications had developed which had left her housebound.

Finally, the vicar approached the graveside and proceeded to quickly go through his well-practiced committal service. It was when he said,

"As we now lay the body of Jennifer in her final resting place beside her beloved father George," I felt a true pang of sadness that left me almost unaware of the rest of the proceedings.

CHAPTER 39

I now sit in my chair, alone, the weeks have passed; weeks of increasing loneliness and lack of purpose. The family hardly come to see me now, or even call, why should they? I didn't make a fuss and simply shared Jennifer's insurance pay-out equally between them, now they have money of their own, what purpose would they have to visit?

I have a daily routine of cleaning the house, making sure that everything is how Jennifer would have liked. I haven't yet begun to empty wardrobes or draws of her stuff, it all seems a little too soon, the thoughts of the last vestiges of her life being rummaged through in a charity shop or a jumble sale seems undignified.

I go into work as little as possible, it's a big surprise to me that the business continues to function perfectly without me; what was my purpose there? was my presence ever of any consequence or importance? The world continues to turn, the sun continues to rise and fall, daily life continues in its repetitive circle.

I have too much time to think and the more I think, the more depressed I become, until finally a new cycle of emotions begin with the death of Edith. I thought I would be elated at this news, but quite the opposite. Like the death of Jennifer, I had believed it was my obligation, my destiny, my reward for the years of deceit and betrayal to kill them both with my own hands; I had now been deprived even of this. What was God's purpose? The answer was clear and immediate.

It was Meals on Wheels that had been the route cause of both Edith and Jennifer's sins, they had led them into the temptation of serving both George and myself a regular diet of shepherd's pie, liver and onions, macaroni and cheese, to mention but a few of the poisonous dishes. It was Meals on Wheels that had killed Jennifer, they were responsible for her being present on that street, on that fateful day when the car had knocked her down. Other than the demise of Mrs Fletcher and Mrs Gladstone, Meals on Wheels had not suffered even the slightest of inconvenience, they had not paid for their responsibility for Jennifer death. They certainly had not paid the price for failing the clients in their community by serving such appalling food to them and of course, the husbands and families of this stout brigade of deceitful women. They all needed to pay for their sins.

My malaise has been replaced by an ever-growing anger and a cold, focused desire for revenge had finally raised me from my chair. I realised I had been given a mission and felt a new and real purpose to my life.

CHAPTER 40

Diary note:

Although I no longer have need to make diary notes to record my emotions or feelings, as suggested on the Personal Development Course, I believe that it is still a useful means of recording plans and events, particularly with my new mission being of such importance, and the need to apply meticulous attention to detail to ensure its complete success.

I have re-established my routine at work and am sitting at my desk, Jennifer has brought me a coffee and two chocolate digestives. She's wearing trousers today, I think I may have to speak with her about that as they cover one of her best assets.

Tomorrow, which is Wednesday, 'my weekly cycling day', I have everything prepared and the 'Reverend Philip Chambers', alias 'The Reverend Martin Entwistle', will be commencing his programme of revenge. I have some new little twists to my previous efforts, which include leaving little notes with new recipes and menu suggestions.

Can't wait, must go home and have an early night so I'll be at my best.

THE END.

Printed in Great Britain
by Amazon